The Little
Big Book for **God's
Children**

This book belongs to:

_____

_____

_____

Published in 2001 by Welcome Books,
An imprint of Welcome Enterprises, Inc.
588 Broadway, Suite 303, New York, NY 10012
(212) 343-9430 Fax (212) 343-9434
email: info@wepub.com
www.wepub.com

Project Director: Alice Wong
Project Assistant: Lawrence Chesler
Editorial Research: Kathleen King, Nicholas Liu

Bible stories retold by Wendy Wax
Parables retold by Wendy Wax and Nicholas Liu
Aesop's fables retold by Monique Peterson
Activities by Monique Peterson and Alice Wong
Music arrangement by Frank Zuback

Distributed to the trade in the U.S. and Canada by
Andrews McMeel Distribution Services
Order Department and Customer Service (800) 826-4216
Orders Only Fax: (800) 437-8683

Library of Congress Control Number: 2001 132593

Printed in Singapore
First Edition
3 5 7 9 10 8 6 4 2

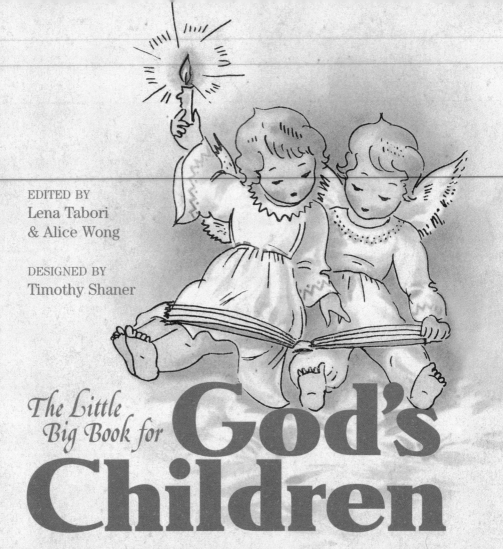

EDITED BY
Lena Tabori
& Alice Wong

DESIGNED BY
Timothy Shaner

The Little
Big Book for God's
Children

WELCOME BOOKS
New York • San Francisco

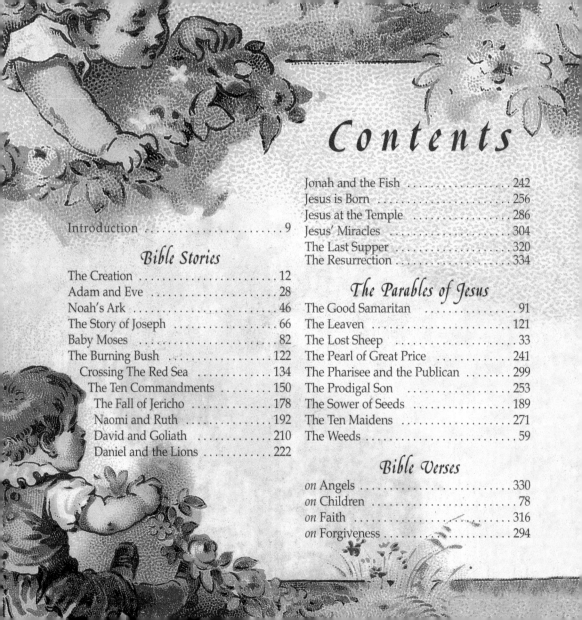

Contents

Prayers

Poetry

Activities

Introduction

hildren are blessings from God. We have so many hopes and dreams for them but simply, we want them to grow strong in mind, body, and spirit. As parents, we love, clothe, feed, and educate them. As Christians, we teach them about God and faith.

This book is our gift to you and your family. Open to any page and find words and illustrations that will uplift your spirit. The bible stories, verses, and parables presented are familiar and comforting for all ages. Aesop's fables and writings by Oscar Wilde, Leo Tolstoy, and James Baldwin reinforce christian ideas. From Joyce Kilmer's simple tribute in "Trees" to Shel Silverstein's humorous "Ma and God", renowned poets are inspiring in their homage to the Lord. And, because voices lifted in song and prayer is a wondrous thing, there are over 20 favorite hymns and spirituals, as well as numerous prayers of thanks, praise, and guidance. Finally, for the little ones, fun activities such as creating a nativity scene, Noah's ark, and Joseph's coat are included.

The bible teaches us about faith, mercy, forgiveness, prayer, love of neighbor, nature, and all of God's creatures. *The Little Big Book for God's Children* explores these and other Christian teachings through the different materials presented. The parable of the good samaritan is followed by Isaac Watts' poem "Kind Deeds" and a story by Leo Tolstoy. The bible story of Jonah learning to answer God's call is reinforced by the hymn "Here I Am Lord". Bible verses on song and praise are emphasized by Aesop's fable of the caged finch faithfully singing his song, St. Francis of Assisi's "Praised Be My Lord", and an activity for making tambourines and harps. Savor this book page by page.

We hope that you and your family will sit together and enjoy this beautiful book inspired by the wisdom of the Bible and the beauty of God's creation. And, like the rich soil in the parable of the sower, we hope that it will help your children grow vibrantly and blossom as children of God.

Are we not
all children
of one Father?

MALACHI 2:10

The Creation

In the beginning, there was no world at all. No sun, no moon, no day, no night, no men, no women, no children. There was just God and darkness and the sounds of raging waters.

"Let there be light!" God said, and in no time (since there wasn't even time yet), warm, bright light appeared, chasing every bit of darkness away. God called the light "day" and the dark "night." Night would follow day, and day would follow night.

"It's good," God said, "but I'm not finished yet."

Night passed, day came. In the bright light all God could see was water—water above, water below, and water in between. Too much water and too little of anything else.

"Let there be a wide space where no waters flow!" God said, and suddenly a clear blue expanse broke through the waters, above and around. God called it "sky" and adorned it with white puffs called "clouds." The clouds held droplets of water so that God could cleanse all that lay below with a shower.

"It's good," God said, as the second day came to an end, "but I'm not finished yet."

Night passed, day came. God gazed down at the giant waves below the clear, blue sky. "There's still too much water!" he said, watching the waves rock back and forth, back and forth.

"Let there be dry places among all this wetness!" God said, and then and there dark, dry patches began to poke up through the waters. God called these dry areas "land," and he called the waters, which now rolled onto sandy beaches, "seas." And that wasn't all . . . .

"Let plants and trees grow on the land!" God said. Instantly, the land looked as if a can of green paint had spilled over it. Green grass, green trees, green bushes . . . and soon other colorful vegetation appeared. There were cornstalks, grapevines, blueberry bushes, daisies, wild strawberries, and multicolored tulips carpeting the land.

"It's good," God said, as the third day came to an end, "but I'm not finished yet."

Night passed, day came. "Night is dark, day is light—but there is no in-between," God said, thoughtfully. And with no in-between, there was no way to tell what time of day or night it was.

"Let there be two great lights in

13

the sky to separate day from night!" God said, and that's when the sun and the moon came into being. The sun ruled day and the moon ruled night. Now there was a way to keep track of weeks, months, seasons, years, decades, and centuries.

"Since the sun is the brighter light," God said, "it shall come and go with grand style." He gathered every shade of red, blue, yellow, purple, and orange and whipped them into a dazzling sunrise and a brilliant sunset. God found them so beautiful, he continued making sunrise after sunrise, sunset after sunset, until he could be sure no two of them would

ever be alike. Then he made trillions of twinkling stars to shine around the moon so it wouldn't be lonesome.

"It's good," God said, as the fourth day came to an end, "but I'm not finished yet."

Night passed, day came. God looked down at the seas, then up at the sky. "So much space and so little in it!" God said. It was much too empty and silent.

"Let the seas and sky be filled with living creatures!" God said, and suddenly the silence broke into millions of sounds. Hummingbirds hummed, sparrows chirped, woodpeckers pecked, doves cooed, hawks screeched, geese honked, and billions of wings

fluttered in the sky above, while fish splashed, dolphins sang, crabs crept, frogs croaked, and whales tooted in the seas below.

"It's good," God said, as the fifth day came to an end, "but I'm not finished yet."

Night passed, day came. God listened to a crow cawing in the sky above as he watched a minnow dart through shallow water. Suddenly, he noticed that the shallow water was filled with green leaves, vines, and roots. He looked up and noticed how quickly the plants, trees, and other vegetation were growing.

"Let the land be filled with living

creatures," God said. "There is plenty for them to eat!" Instantly, the land was filled with roaring lions, buzzing bees, creeping lizards, scampering mice, growling bears, laughing hyenas, squealing pigs, wandering camels, slithering snakes, stomping elephants, waddling penguins, and many other animals. And that wasn't all. . . .

"Let there be someone just like me to care for the living creatures on land, in the sky, and in the seas!" God said, scooping up a handful of dust. He blew on it, and a man appeared before him—the first man in the world!

The Creation

The man squinted in the sunlight as he looked at God, and then at the world around him, with awe.

"I shall call you 'Adam,'" God said.

"Then Adam I am," the man said with a smile. He watched as God blew on another handful of dust to create a woman.

"What shall you call her?" Adam asked God.

"I'll leave that up to you," God said.

"I'll call you 'Eve,'" Adam said to the woman ("Eve" means "living").

"Then Eve I am," said the woman.

"You shall have lots of children," God said to them. "Teach them to take care of the world and the living creatures in it, for it is a very special place."

"We will," Adam and Eve promised.

"It's good," God said, as the sixth day came to an end. "And now I am finished. Tomorrow I shall rest!"

On the seventh day, while the sun shined high in the sky, and the daisies grew taller, and the horses galloped through the woods, and robins laid eggs in nests, and giraffes chomped on leafy treetops, and rabbits dug holes to live in, and fish swam in schools, and polar bears trod across ice, and monkeys swung from branch to branch, and Adam and Eve talked in the shade, God was peacefully asleep.

The Creation

by Cecil Francis Alexander

All things bright and beautiful,
    All creatures, great and small,
All things wise and wonderful,
    The Lord God made them all.

Each little flower that opens,
    Each little bird that sings,
He made their glowing colors,
    He made their tiny wings;

The rich man in his castle,
    The poor man at his gate,
God made them, high or lowly,
    And ordered their estate.

The purple-headed mountain,
    The river running by,
The sunset and the morning,
    That brightens up the sky;

The cold wind in the winter,
    The pleasant summer sun,
The ripe fruits in the garden—
    He made them every one.

The tall trees in the greenwood,
    The meadows where we play,
The rushes by the water
    We gather every day,—

He gave us eyes to see them,
    And lips that we might tell
How great is God Almighty,
    Who has made all things well!

And God saw every thing
that he had made, and,
behold, it was very good.

GENESIS 1:31

Morning Prayer

by Ogden Nash

Now another day is breaking,
Sleep was sweet and so is waking.
Dear Lord, I promised you last night
Never again to sulk or fight.
Such vows are easier to keep
When a child is sound asleep.
Today, O Lord, for your dear sake,
I'll try to keep them when I wake.

Morning Has Broken

Words by Eleanor Farjeon

Morn - ing has bro - ken like the first morn - ing;

Black - bird has spo - ken like the first bird. _____

Praise for the sing - ing, praise for the morn - ing,

Praise for them spring - ing fresh from the word. _____

2. Mine is the sunlight, mine is the morning,
   Born of the one light Eden saw play.
   Praise with elation, praise ev'ry morning,
   God's re-creation of the new day.

24

God's Creatures

How many are your works, O Lord! In wisdom you made them all; the earth is full of your creatures.

PSALM 104:24

H*elp your children feed and care for God's creatures. Maybe you'll make some new friends or witness the miracle of a caterpillar becoming a butterfly.*

Bird Feeder

plastic gallon jug, scissors, wire hanger, birdseed

1. Cut a 5-inch circle out of the side of the jug, 2 inches from the bottom.
2. Untwist hanger and poke wire through the top of jug. Twist ends together.
3. Fill with birdseed to edge of hole. Hang on tree.

Corn Stake Feeder

piece of wood (12 x 4 inches), galvanized nails, corn

1. Drive a row of nails through the board, about 3 inches apart. Slide an ear of corn on each nail.
2. Put the feeder outdoors for squirrels, chipmunks, or rabbits.

Incubate a Butterfly

glass jar, caterpillar, leaves, wax paper, rubber band

1. Go on a caterpillar hunt during the spring and early summer. Look for one about the size of your little finger on trees. Carefully transfer it to your jar.
2. Cut a few small branches from the tree you found the caterpillar on and set aside in some water.
3. Cut a twig with several leaves from your branches and add to jar.
4. Cover the jar opening with wax paper. Seal it with a rubber band and poke several holes.
5. Give the caterpillar fresh leaves regularly.
6. The caterpillar will form a chrysalis and hatch in a few weeks. Gently ease it into the open air and watch your butterfly spread its wings.

Adam and Eve

od had created a beautiful world with one especially pretty place called Eden. Eden had sweeter-smelling flowers, greener plants, shadier trees, tastier fruits, and friendlier animals than any other place on earth. God chose this wonderful garden to be Adam and Eve's home, for he wanted them to be comfortable and happy.

"You may do as you like in Eden," God said, "as long as you follow one rule."

"Anything you say," Adam said to God.

God gestured toward two trees in the middle of the garden. "This is the Tree of Life," he said, pointing to one of them. "Anyone who eats its fruit will live forever and ever." Then he pointed to the other tree. "This is the Tree of Knowledge. Anyone who eats its fruit will know good and evil."

"What is the rule you'd like us to obey?" Eve asked.

"You must never, never, never eat fruit from the Tree of Knowledge," God said. "Don't even touch it or you will die."

Adam and Eve promised God they would never eat fruit from the Tree of Knowledge. It seemed like an easy rule to follow, especially as there was plenty of other fruit around.

So Adam and Eve settled into their new home. They spent the days strolling through the garden, wading in shallow brooks, making friends with animals, listening to birdcalls, gathering food, and picnicking under shady trees. At night, they lay under the stars, falling asleep to a chorus of chirping crickets. They were always naked, the way God created them, and never had a reason to be ashamed or afraid. They were good and they knew God loved them.

One day, Eve was gathering nuts near the Tree of Knowledge when a serpent crossed her path. What Eve didn't know was that the serpent was sneakier than the other animals.

"Is it true that God told you not to eat from the Tree of Knowledge?" the serpent asked.

"Yes," said Eve. "He said we would die if we touched it."

"And you believed him?" hissed the serpent.

Eve nodded innocently.

Adam and Eve

"God is just trying to protect you from knowing the difference between good and evil," the serpent hissed. "But don't you think you have a right to know the difference? God does, so why shouldn't you?"

Eve turned to the Tree of Knowledge and, for the first time, looked closely at its ripe, red fruit. She wondered whether it was sweet or sour.

"Don't you want to know all that God knows?" the serpent teased.

"Well...I am curious," Eve said, her mouth starting to water. And before she could stop herself, she plucked the fruit from the branch and took a small bite. It tasted stranger than the other fruits in the garden. "I'll give Adam a taste," she said, turning back toward the serpent—but it had disappeared.

Eve found Adam playing with a family of monkeys. "Here, Adam," she said, holding out the fruit. "Taste this. It's from the Tree of Knowledge."

"But we promised God..." Adam began.

"I know," Eve said, "but aren't you just a bit curious?"

Adam bit into the fruit.

Suddenly, a cold wind swept over them though the sun still shone brightly in the sky. Shivering, they tried to cover up their nakedness with fig leaves. For the first time in their lives they were afraid, and they

Adam and Eve

could hear God approaching!

"Let's hide!" Adam said, pulling Eve behind a tree. But it was no use hiding from God. When he saw them covering up their naked bodies and shivering in the cold, he knew they had disobeyed him.

"Have you eaten the fruit from the Tree of Knowledge?" God asked Adam.

"Y-yes," Adam said, bowing his head. "Eve gave it to me."

"Is that true?" God said, looking at Eve.

"Yes," Eve said, bowing her head. "The serpent tricked me."

Though God still loved Adam and Eve, he had to punish them. "I must now forbid you from eating fruit from the Tree of Life," he said sadly. "You

shall not live forever and ever as I will."

"We'll obey you this time!" Adam and Eve said to God.

"That's what you said the last time," God said, "and you went back on your word. Just to be sure you don't disobey me this time, you must leave Eden—permanently."

So clinging to each other with their heads bowed, Adam and Eve went into the large, unfamiliar world. Would they find enough food? How would they protect themselves from dangerous animals? Would they know a poisonous plant if they saw one? The only things they were sure of were that God still loved them and that there was no turning back.

The Lost Sheep

Once upon a time, there was a shepherd who had one hundred sheep. One day, on the way home from the pastures where the sheep grazed, one of the sheep became lost. The shepherd waited and waited, but the one lost sheep did not return. Finally, he decided to leave his ninety-nine sheep to search for the one lost lamb.

He looked everywhere, in every nook and cranny, high up in the mountains and low down near the seas, calling its name, "Sheep! Sheep! Where are you, sheep?" After days of searching, the shepherd finally came to a cave. He heard a faint baaaa, baaaa coming from inside the cave. It was the lost sheep, hiding in fear, hoping to be saved. The shepherd hugged the sheep in joy and put him on his shoulders. He carried it home, singing all the way.

Upon reaching home, he called all his neighbors to his house for a party to celebrate. This is the way, too, in heaven. There will be more joy over saving one lost soul than over ninety-nine who never strayed.

> *Rejoice with me;*
> *I have found my*
> *lost sheep.*
>
> LUKE 15:6

33

God bless all those that I love;
God bless all those that love me:
God bless all those that love those that I love
And all those that love those that love me.

Amen.

Dear Father, hear and bless
Thy beasts and singing birds,
And guard with tenderness
Small things that have no words.

Amen.

The Cat, the Mouse, and the Rooster

A young mouse, which hadn't seen much of the world, came home one day and said, "Oh, I've had such a fright! I've seen a thing with such a fierce look, that struts here and there on two legs. On his head, he wears a small red flag, and one round his throat, too. He flaps his arms at his sides as if he should rise in the air. You should have seen him stretch out his head and roar at me with his sharp mouth. I thought he would eat me up! I shook from head to foot with fear, and I was glad to run home as fast as my feet would carry me. If it weren't for that horrible creature, I would've made friends with the sweetest soul. She had soft fur like ours, which was black and gray in streaks. Her look was so meek that I fell quite in love with her. She had a fine long tail, which she waved to and fro. When I saw her fix her bright eyes on me I thought she had a wish to speak. But that fierce wretch crowed his scream, which drove me here, quite out of breath with fear."

"Ah!" said the old mouse, "it was good you ran for your life, but the fierce creature was not your enemy. It was a rooster that wouldn't have harmed you in the least. That sweet thing, of which you seem so fond, was a cat, and cats eat us mice all the time!"

Judge not by looks.

37

The Sermon
to the Birds

Retold by James Baldwin

ery kind and loving was St. Francis—kind and loving not only to men but to all living things. He spoke of the birds as his little brothers of the air, and he could never bear to see them harmed.

At Christmastime he scattered crumbs of bread under the trees, so that the tiny creatures could feast and be happy.

Once when a boy gave him a pair of doves which he had snared, St. Francis had a nest made for them, and the mother bird laid her eggs in it.

By and by, the eggs hatched, and a nestful of young doves grew up. they were so tame that they sat on the shoulders of St. Francis and ate from his hand.

And many other stories are told of this man's great love and pity for the timid creatures which lived in the fields and woods.

The Sermon to the Birds

One day as he was walking among the trees the birds saw him and flew down to greet him. They sang their sweetest songs to show how much they loved him. Then, when they saw that he was about to speak, they nestled softly in the grass and listened.

"O little birds," he said, "I love you, for you are my brothers and sisters of the air. Let me tell you something, my little brothers, my little sisters: You ought always to love God and praise Him.

"For think what He has given you. He has given you wings with which to fly through the air. He has given you clothing both warm and beautiful. He has given you the air in which to move and have homes.

"And think of this, O little brothers: you sow not, neither do you reap, for God feeds you. He gives you the rivers and the brooks from which to drink. He gives you the mountains and the valleys where you may rest. He gives you the trees in which to build your nests.

"You toil not, neither do you spin, yet God takes care of you and your little ones. It must be, then, that He loves you. So, do not be ungrateful, but sing His praises and thank Him for his goodness toward you."

Then the saint stopped speaking and looked around him. All the birds sprang up joyfully. They spread their wings and opened their mouths to show that they understood his words.

And when he had blessed them, all began to sing; and the whole forest was filled with sweetness and joy because of their wonderful melodies.

Hurt No Living Thing

by Christina Rossetti

Hurt no living thing;
    Ladybird, nor butterfly,
    Nor moth with dusty wing,
Nor cricket chirping cheerily,
Nor grasshopper so light of leap,
    Nor dancing gnat, nor beetle fat,
    Nor harmless worms that creep.

Praise God, from Whom All Blessings Flow

Praise God, from whom all bless - ings flow. Praise

God, all crea - tures here be - low. Cre - -

a - tor, Sav - ior, Spir - it praise. In

joy - ful song through all our days. Praise

Noah's Ark

any, many years passed after Adam and Eve had left Eden. They had had lots of children, and now had grandchildren, great grandchildren, and great great grandchildren! God hoped the offspring of Adam and Eve would respect the earth and care for the animals, but it turned out they did no such thing. Instead, these people became mean and selfish, and often acted in horrible ways. They had stopped listening to God.

"I'm sorry I ever created these people," God said, sadly. "I shall destroy the world and start over." But first he went to see a man named Noah.

Noah was six hundred years old and had three sons, Shem, Ham, and Jepheth. Noah was kind and honest, and he always obeyed God.

"Noah," God said, when he found him. "I plan to cause a huge flood to wash over the earth. Everyone will drown—except for you and your family and some animals."

Noah listened carefully as God told him what to do.

"Build an ark of wood with large rooms inside, and be sure to seal all the cracks with pitch to keep the water out," God instructed. Then he gave him the exact measurements of the wood. "It will have three decks, a window near the top, and a door on the side.

"When the seas begin to rise, this ark will be a safe place for you and your wife, your three sons and their wives."

"I'll do as you say," Noah said, grateful that he and his family were to be spared.

"But why do we need such a large ark?"

"Because you are to bring with you two of each living creature, one male and one female, so that they can multiply in the new world. And you'll need lots of food, too."

Noah rounded up his sons and they got right to work. They measured and hammered, sawed and sanded, and soon the ark began to take shape.

"What a stupid thing to make," a neighbor said to Noah.

"What do you expect from such a crazy old man?" said another neighbor.

But Noah didn't listen to any of them. He listened only to God.

When the ark was finally finished, Noah and his sons rounded up the animals. Then, at last, they were ready to board the ark.

First, Noah led his family up the wooden plank that led to the highest deck. Next came the animals, two by two. Grrrrrr. Grrrrr. Cluck. Cluck. Stomp. Stomp. Quack. Quack. Ruff. Ruff. Neigh. Neigh. Tweet. Tweet. Squeak! Squeak! Mooo! Mooo!

Wh-ish. Wh-ish. Cheep. Cheep. Snort. Snort. Oink. Oink. Hiss! Hiss! Meow! Meow! Hyenas, goats, peacocks, zebras, turtles, camels, giraffes, doves, hippopotami, pheasants, bears, penguins, donkeys, lizards, rabbits, frogs, buffalo, sheep, and every other animal imaginable climbed aboard with its mate. Some had spots, some were striped, some were huge, some were tiny, some were loud, some were quiet...what a magnificent parade!

"They'll never be able to drag that boat to the sea," a neighbor said, having no idea about the floods. "It's much too heavy." The other neighbors laughed.

Just as Noah and his sons pulled up the wooden plank the sky grew cloudy. Then it began to sprinkle.

By the time they showed the pigs to their sty near the middle deck, the horses to their stables near the upper deck, the chickens to their coops near the front of the ark, the kittens to their basket near the back of the ark, and the other animals to their own special areas, the rain started coming down.

Pitter-patter, pitter-patter. The drops splattered against the shutters of the window near the top of the boat.

Pitter-patter, pitter-patter. The drops splattered against the window shutters of a nearby house where people were pushing and shoving for

a place to look out. They all wanted to watch the ark as puddles formed around it.

B-O-OOM! Thunder crashed. Lightning flashed. The rain pounded and poured as the wind picked up strength and speed. On land, roofs began to leak, puddles poured into other puddles, and people grew frantic. Noah's ark no longer seemed like such a bad idea to them. For forty days and forty nights, it rained and poured. Puddles became rivers and rivers became seas. The ark tossed and turned as giant waves crashed thousands of feet in the air! The last of the rooftops and treetops and mountaintops had long since disappeared beneath the floods. But Noah, his family, and the animals were safe and dry inside the ark.

At the end of the fortieth day, the rain suddenly stopped. Everything was silent and still, and the ark rocked gently in the water.

Noah hurried to the window and gasped. All he saw was water—water everywhere. Not a house or tree or mountain in sight! "God has done what he set out to do," he announced to the others. "The old world is gone forever!"

Then he beckoned to a raven.

The raven left its mate and flew over to Noah.

"Fly out to look for dry land," Noah said to the raven. "When you find it, come back and show us the way."

After the raven flew out the window, Noah flung open the door and led his wife, and then his sons and their wives, onto the upper deck of the ark. Next came two panthers, then two pandas, then two crocodiles, two blue jays, and two swans. Soon all three decks were completely full!

It had been so long since they had been outside, and the fresh air felt wonderful! Two days later the raven returned. It looked tired and hungry—and it hadn't found an inch of land. It hadn't even found a place to perch!

Next, Noah sent out a dove. The dove was gone for many months and finally returned with an olive leaf in its beak.

"The water must be going down!" Noah said. "The land is finally drying up!"

After a hearty meal and a good night's cuddle with its mate, the dove flew out again. While it was gone, the waters got lower and lower until small islands, and then larger pieces of land, began to poke through. This time, the dove didn't return—but no one seemed to mind.

Noah's Ark

"It's time to leave the ark," God said to Noah one day. "Bring your wife, and your sons and their wives, and bring every pair of animals so they can have lots of babies. Welcome to the new world!"

When they drifted onto land, Noah and his sons set up the wooden plank and two by two the animals left the ark. The tigers prowled down the plank. The chickens scrambled down the plank. The elephants climbed down the plank. The ducks waddled down the plank. The puppies scurried down the plank. The horses galloped down the plank. The canaries fluttered down the plank. The mice scampered down the plank. The cows roamed down the plank. The worms wiggled down the plank. The monkeys swung down the plank. The bulls charged down the plank. The pigs scuffled down the plank. The snakes slithered down the plank. The kittens pattered down the plank. And all the other animals followed behind them.

Next came Noah's sons and their wives.

And last, Noah and his wife came down the plank. It felt strange to walk on dry land, for they had been on the ark for so long!

Noah and his family sat on the ground and thanked God for taking care of them.

When God heard their thanks, he gave them a beautiful gift in the sky— a dazzling rainbow, the first ever.

The Prayer of the Little Ducks

by Carmen Bernos de Gasztold

Dear God,
give us a flood of water.
Let it rain tomorrow and always.
Give us plenty of little slugs
and other luscious things to eat.
Protect all folk who quack
and everyone who knows how to swim.

                              Amen.

Noah's Ark

You are to bring

into the ark two of

all living creatures,

male and female,

to keep them alive

with you.

GENESIS 6:19

The next time it rains, imagine with your children what it must have been like for Noah and all the animals on the ark while it rained for forty days and nights! Then get busy and make an ark of your own, complete with animals. How many animals can you make before the rain stops?

Shoebox Ark

cardboard shoebox, markers, scissors, popsicle sticks, glue

1. Draw door and windows on the sides of the box and cut along their outlines. Leave a hinge of cardboard on the door so it can open and close. The door should also be about an inch from the bottom of the box.
2. Lay 3 or 4 popsicle sticks together to make a plank. Break 2 or 3 popsicle sticks in half and glue them across the plank to hold it in place.
3. Decorate the ark with markers. You can draw lines to indicate strips of wood or add rolling blue waves to the bottom of the ark.

Two by Two

flour, salt, water, food coloring, toothpicks, seeds, rice, sequins, notions

1. Mix one part flour, two parts salt, and two parts water in a bowl until the consistency is like clay.
2. Separate the dough into several balls. Add a different food coloring to each ball for a variety of colors.
3. Create animal bodies by rolling chunks of clay into little balls. Make smaller balls for heads. Use toothpicks to reinforce legs, giraffe necks, or elephant trunks. Add seeds for eyes, wild rice for porcupine quills, or sequins for leopard spots.
4. Let dry for a few days.

The Weeds

The kingdom of heaven is like the man who sowed his field with good seed. While the man slept, his enemy came, sowed weeds among the wheat, and then ran away. When the wheat began to sprout and grow, the weeds began to sprout and grow along with it.

The man's servants came to him and said, "Sir, didn't you sow good seed in your field?"

"Yes, I did," said the man.

"Then where did the weeds come from?" they asked.

"My enemy must have planted them," the man replied.

"Do you want us to pull out all the weeds?" his servants asked.

"No," the man answered, "because while you are pulling up the weeds, you might pull up some of the wheat, too. Let the wheat and the weeds grow together until the harvest. At that time, I will tell the harvesters to gather the weeds, tie them into bundles, and burn them. When that's done, I'll tell them to gather the wheat and bring it into my barn."

Someday, the angels will be like the harvesters, looking across the lands under heaven, separating the good from the bad.

> *The kingdom of heaven is like a man who sowed good seed in his field.*
>
> MATTHEW 13:24

59

Do Lord

I've got a home in glo - ry land that (clap) out-shines the

sun, (Oh, Lord - y) I've got a home in glo - ry land that

(clap) out - shines the sun. I've got a home in

glo - ry land that (clap) out - shines the sun, Look a - - -

way be - yond ___ the blue. ___

Do Lord, oh, do Lord, oh do re-mem-ber me, (Oh, Lord-y),

Do Lord, oh, do Lord, oh, do re-mem-ber me,

Do Lord, oh do Lord, oh, do re-mem-ber me, Look a -

way be - yond___ the blue._____

Prayers

Please give me what I ask, dear Lord,
If you'd be glad about it,
But if you think it's not for me,
Please help me do without it.

                    Amen.

Lord, teach me all that I should know;
In grace and wisdom I may grow;
The more I learn to do Thy will,
The better may I love Thee still.

                    Isaac Watts

The Story of Joseph

any years ago, in a place called Hebron, a shepherd named Jacob had twelve sons. His favorite was his eleventh son, Joseph. For this reason, Joseph's older brothers were jealous of him—especially when their father made him a beautiful coat. The coat was embroidered with intricate patterns of purple, red, blue, and yellow, and Joseph wore it everywhere.

One night, Joseph had a strange dream that seemed real. The next morning, he put on his special coat and raced out to the pasture to tell his brothers about it. (Joseph liked his brothers even though they were mean to him.)

"Those bright colors might scare away the flock," said Reuben, the oldest brother, when he saw Joseph still a mile away.

"He's too in love with himself to care," said Judah.

"Brothers!" Joseph said breathlessly, as he approached. "Last night I dreamt we were all out in the pasture tying grain into bundles. My bundle leapt out of my arms and stood straight up in front of me. Then all your bundles leapt out of your hands, formed a circle around my bundle, and bowed down to it."

"You're not a king!" Judah said angrily.

"We'd never bow down to you!" said Simon.

But Joseph ignored his brothers' nastiness—he was used to it.

A few days later, Joseph had

another dream. Again he put on his coat of many colors and went to tell his brothers.

"Last night I dreamt that the sun and the moon and eleven stars were bowing down to me," he said, smiling.

"We have better things to do than listen to your silly dreams," his brothers yelled angrily.

But when Joseph told his father about the dream, Jacob didn't think it was silly at all. Could I be the sun, my wife Rachel the moon, and my eleven other sons the stars that bow down to Joseph in the dream, he wondered?

One day, Jacob sent his oldest sons and their flocks to a far-off pasture where he had heard grass and water were plentiful. A few days later, he sent Joseph to check on them.

Joseph climbed hill after hill, and crossed valley after valley, until he finally saw his brothers and their flocks in the distance.

"There's that colorful coat again," Judah said to his brothers.

"Let's kill him so we won't have to listen to his silly dreams," said Levi.

"I have a better idea," said Reuben. "Let's dig a hole, throw him in, and leave him to die alone." The others liked this idea even better, not knowing that Reuben secretly planned to rescue Joseph when they weren't looking. Being the oldest brother he felt responsible—and he knew it was wrong to kill.

They quickly dug a deep hole and waited. When Joseph approached, they grabbed him, tore off his colorful coat, and threw him into the hole.

"LET ME OUT OF HERE!" Joseph cried. "HE-E-ELP!"

Later in the day, a caravan of merchants came by on their way to Egypt to sell spices.

"Let's sell Joseph to the merchants," Judah said to his brothers. "After all, he is our brother and leaving him in the hole to die is a bit harsh." The others agreed and quickly fetched Joseph from the hole. They sold him for twenty shekels of silver.

"What shall we tell our father?" Judah said guiltily. "He'll want to know where his favorite son is."

After much thought they decided to slaughter a goat and dip Joseph's coat in its blood. And that's just what they did.

"Look what we found!" Reuben said to their father when they returned to Hebron. "Isn't this the coat you made for Joseph?"

As Jacob examined the coat his eyes filled with tears. "Yes, indeed, this is my eleventh son's coat," he said sadly. "A ferocious animal must have eaten him." He then spent many days mourning for Joseph.

Meanwhile, Joseph arrived in Egypt and was sold as a slave to a rich man named Potiphar. As soon as Joseph met Potiphar, he knew God was taking care of him, for Potiphar was very kind. Instead of making Joseph build pyramids in the hot sun, Potiphar gave him an easy job in the palace. "Make sure the maids keep the house clean and the cook prepares good meals," he said. And that's just what Joseph did for many years—always making sure to do a good job so that God would be happy.

One day, while Potiphar was out of town, Potiphar's wife noticed how handsome Joseph had become. "Come to my bedroom," she said to him.

Now, most men would have gone, for Potiphar's wife was very beautiful, but Joseph just shook his head. "You're very pretty," he said, "but it would not be right."

Feeling hurt and rejected, she ripped Joseph's cloak and took it from him. When Potiphar returned, his wife showed him the torn cloak and told him that Joseph had attacked her—of course, this was a lie. Potiphar believed his wife and had Joseph thrown into prison.

As a prisoner, Joseph kept his cell clean, shared his food with the other prisoners, and prayed to God to set him free. When the other prisoners had strange dreams, they relied on Joseph to tell them what they meant.

"Thank you, Joseph," they would say. "Don't thank me, thank God," he would answer them.

One time, Joseph told a prisoner that his dream meant he'd be rescued in three days. When the dream came true, Joseph said, "Please mention me to the Pharaoh." (You see, the prisoner was the Pharaoh's cup bearer—the one responsible for keeping his wine cup full.)

One night, after Joseph had been in prison for two years, the Pharaoh had a confusing dream. In the morning, he called for his wise men and told them his dream. "Tell me what it means," he said to them.

But though they checked their charts and scrolls, the wise men couldn't help him.

"I know someone who can tell you what your dream means," the Pharaoh's cup bearer said, for he remembered his promise to Joseph over two years before. "His name is Joseph, and he's in prison."

"Then free him!" the Pharaoh ordered. "And bring him to me at once!"

"Can you tell me what my dream means?" the Pharaoh asked Joseph, when he stood before him in fresh, clean clothes.

"I can't," said Joseph, "but God can. What did you dream?"

"In my dream, seven fat cows came out of the River Nile. Then seven thin cows came out of the river and ate the fat cows. But when they finished eating, they were just as thin as before. Then I had another dream. Seven pieces of healthy grain were growing on a single stalk. Soon, seven withered pieces of grain sprouted and swallowed the healthy grain. What does it mean?"

"Please, God," Joseph prayed silently. "What does it mean?" And suddenly he knew, for God had a way of opening Joseph's mind.

"Pharaoh," Joseph said, "both dreams mean the same thing. There will be plenty to eat and drink during the next seven years. But during the seven years after that, the crops won't grow and everyone will go hungry—unless something is done about it."

"Your God really is with you!" the Pharaoh said, truly amazed. "I trust you more than I trust anyone else. From now on, you will rule my palace and make sure that plenty of food is put in storage so that no one will starve when the crops stop growing. You will be the greatest man in Egypt, except for myself, of course."

Joseph couldn't believe his ears! Only a few hours earlier he had been a prisoner and now he was asked to rule over Egypt alongside the Pharaoh! Joseph knew he had only God to thank for this.

Sure enough, the Pharaoh's dream did come true. And when hard times came, Joseph handed out the food that he'd been storing for seven years. When people in other lands heard that there was food in Egypt, they went there hoping to have some for themselves. Joseph's brothers were among these hungry people.

When Joseph's brothers arrived in Egypt, they bowed before the governor of the land—whom they didn't recognize as their brother Joseph! (He was older and more handsome than they remembered.) Joseph, however, knew his brothers right away and told them who he was. At first his brothers were afraid of him. They remembered his dream from long ago and understood that it had come true—they now really were bowing down to him.

"Brothers, there's nothing to be afraid of!" Joseph said warmly. "I don't blame you for anything. God meant for me to be here!" Then he and his brothers hugged and kissed with forgiveness. Joseph, their brother, had the heart of a king.

Joseph's brothers went home and told their father that his son was alive. Soon after that, the whole family moved to Egypt to be near Joseph.

*

73

Brothers and Sisters

The New Class Books for Sabbath Schools: Second Reading Lessons, c. 1875

ow there is another thing for little folks to regard, and that is, that they should live in peace with their own brothers and sisters. For this is right and good.

For you have all the same father and mother, who provide you with food and clothing. You live in the same house, and perhaps sleep in the same bed; and with each other you eat and drink, and talk and pray.

Should you not then try to be good friends? And if you do not agree ought you not to forgive each other, and so be good friends again?

Avoid giving offense; then you will live in peace. So never take the book or play-thing off your brother or sister without their leave.

And never do to them as you would not like them to do to you. This is called the golden rule, and if you go by it, you will not hurt or tease each other, or fall out about trifling things.

For it is not a pleasant thing to be always falling out. It is much better to live in peace and love. Your parents will be happy to see you do so, and the great God will be pleased too.

And mind one thing: brothers and sisters love you more than any other boys or girls in the world.

He's Got the Whole World

He's got the whole world __ in His hands, __ He's got the

whole world __ in his Hands, __ He's got the

whole world __ in His hands, __ He's got the

whole world in His hands.

2. He's got the little, bitty baby in His hands. . .

3. He's got you and me brother . . .

4. He's got you and me sister . . .

5. He's got everybody here. . .

6. He's got the wind and the rain. . .

7. He's got the sun and the moon . . .

8. He's got the whole world . . .

Therefore, whoever humbles himself like this child is the greatest in the kingdom of heaven.

MATTHEW 18:4

Verses on Children

Let the little children come to me, and
do not hinder them, for the kingdom of
heaven belongs to such as these.

MATTHEW 19:14

Train a child in the way he should go, and
when he is old he will not turn from it.

PROVERBS 22:6

Don't let anyone look down on you
because you are young, but set an example
for the believers in speech, in life, in love,
in faith and in purity.

1 TIMOTHY 4:12

Jewels

When He cometh, when He cometh,
To make up His jewels,
All His Jewels, precious jewels,
His loved and His own,
Like the stars of the morning,
His bright crown adorning,
They shall shine in their beauty,
Bright gems for His crown.

He will gather, He will gather
The gems for His kingdom;
All the pure ones, all the bright ones,
His loved and His own.
Like the stars of the morning,
His bright crown adorning,
They shall shine in their beauty,
Bright gems for His crown.

Little children, little children,
Who love their Redeemer,
Are the jewels, precious jewels,
His loved and His own,
Like the stars of the morning,
His bright crown adorning,
They shall shine in their beauty,
Bright gems for His crown.

Sacred Songs and Solos, compiled by Ira D. Sankey, c. 1890

Baby Moses

oseph's family lived in Egypt for many years and multiplied there. As the generations grew larger and larger, they became known as the Israelites, or people of Israel.

Four hundred years after Joseph's family arrived, a cruel Pharaoh came to rule the land. "There are too many Israelites in Egypt," he warned. "If we don't do something soon, they'll become more powerful than us."

The Egyptians listened as Pharaoh gave them orders.

"Make the people of Israel your slaves!" he commanded. "Have them work till they're too tired to have more children."

The Egyptians obeyed their king—they had no choice! They forced the Israelites to be their slaves and demanded that they make bricks and build with them until their shoulders were sore, their backs ached, and their feet were blistered. But still the people of Israel kept having children.

This made Pharaoh even angrier! "From now on," he commanded, "if an Israelite woman gives birth to a baby boy, he must be killed!"

One day, an Israelite woman gave birth to a beautiful baby boy. For three months, the baby stayed hidden inside while the woman, her husband, their daughter, and their son (who'd been born before the rule) tried to come up with a way to save their youngest family member. They prayed to God to send them an idea.

"I've got it!" the mother said one morning. Her husband and children watched as she wove a basket out of reeds. She then wrapped the tiny baby in soft blankets and placed him in the basket. "Come, Miriam," she said to her daughter. And the two of them walked down to the riverbank.

Miriam watched as her mother placed the basket in the river. "Keep an eye on your baby brother," her mother said.

Miriam hid a good distance away from the riverbank and watched the basket.

"What's that?" said a voice.

Miriam looked up and saw Pharaoh's daughter, a princess, and her servants approaching the riverbank to bathe in the river. The princess had spotted the basket. Miriam watched as one of the servants plucked the basket out of the water and brought it to the princess.

"What a beautiful baby!" she cried, peering into the basket. The baby had kicked off his blankets and was crying with hunger. The princess scooped him out of the basket and rocked him gently. "He has such wise eyes," she said. "He must belong to an Israelite woman."

The princess knew about her father's order to kill all Israelite baby boys. But how could such a precious baby be killed? "I'll keep him for myself," she said. "I must find a nurse who can feed him."

At that moment, Miriam came out of hiding. "Would you like me to get an Israelite woman to care for the baby?" Miriam asked.

"I would like that very much," the princess said, smiling. "Fetch her at once—this baby is very hungry."

Miriam raced home and quickly brought her mother back to the riverbank.

"Can you take care of this baby for me?" the princess asked Miriam's mother. "I will pay you."

"I-I'd love to!" the baby's mother said, trying desperately to hold back tears of joy.

"You can bring him back to me when he's old enough to eat on his own," said the princess. "Then I shall adopt him and see that he has a good education and the life of a prince."

So the baby went back to his family to be nursed and cared for by his real mother. His mother thanked God over and over for listening to her prayers. When the baby was three years old, she brought him to the princess who named him Moses ("Moses" means "drawn out," which was fitting since the princess had drawn him out of the river). One day, Moses would become a very important leader in Egypt.

Jesus Loves the Little Children

Je - sus   loves   the   lit - tle   chil - dren,

All   the   chil - dren   of   the   world,   Red   and

yel - low, black and white, They are   pre - cious in   His sight,   Je - sus

loves   the   lit - tle chil - dren of   the   world.

No Difference

by Shel Silverstein

Small as a peanut,
Big as a giant,
We're all the same size
When we turn off the light.

Rich as a sultan,
Poor as a mite,
We're all worth the same
When we turn off the light.

Red, black or orange,
Yellow or white,
We all look the same
When we turn off the light.

So maybe the way
To make everything right
Is for God to just reach out
And turn off the light!

Ma and God

by Shel Silverstein

God gave us fingers—Ma says, "Use your fork."
God gave us voices—Ma says, "Don't scream."
Ma says eat broccoli, cereal and carrots.
But God gave us tasteys for maple ice cream.

God gave us fingers—Ma says, "Use your hanky."
God gave us puddles—Ma says, "Don't splash."
Ma says, "Be quiet, your father is sleeping."
But God gave us garbage can covers to crash.

God gave us fingers—Ma says, "Put your gloves on."
God gave us raindrops—Ma says, "Don't get wet."
Ma says be careful, and don't get too near to
Those strange lovely dogs that God gave us to pet.

God gave us fingers—Ma says, "Go wash 'em."
But God gave us coal bins and nice dirty bodies.
And I ain't too smart, but there's one thing for certain—
Either Ma's wrong or else God is.

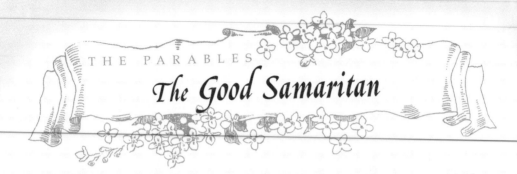

THE PARABLES

The Good Samaritan

A man was walking from Jerusalem to Jericho when robbers attacked him. They stole his money and clothing, beat him, and left him on the side of the road half-dead.

Soon, a priest came along. When he saw the half-dead man lying in the dirt, he crossed to the other side of the road and continued on his way.

Next, a Levite came along. When he saw the half-dead man lying in the dirt, he too crossed to the other side and continued on his way.

Finally, a Samaritan came along. When he saw the half-dead man lying in the dirt, he stopped and felt sad for him. He soaked the man's wounds in oil and wine, put bandages on them, and carefully lifted the man onto his horse. After that, he climbed on the horse with the man and rode to the nearest inn where he looked after the man all night.

The next day, the Samaritan gave the innkeeper two pieces of silver. "Take care of my friend," he said, "and if you need more money, I will give it to you on my journey back." After Jesus told this parable to a lawyer, he asked, "Which of the men acted like a true neighbor to the man at the side of the road?"

"The Samaritan," the lawyer answered.

"Then go and do the same yourself," Jesus replied.

> Love your neighbor as yourself.
>
> LUKE 10:27

Verses on Mercy

If a man shuts his ears to the cry of the poor,
he too will cry out and not be answered.

PROVERBS 21:13

[The righteous] are always generous and
lend freely; their children will be blessed.

PSALM 37:26

Remember this: Whoever sows sparingly
will also reap sparingly, and whoever sows
generously will also reap generously. Each
man should give what he has decided in
his heart to give, not reluctantly or under
compulsion, for God loves a cheerful giver.

2 CORINTHIANS 9:6–7

I tell you the truth, whatever you did not do for one of the least of these, you did not do for me.

MATTHEW 25:45

Kum Ba Yah
(Come By Here)

Kum ba yah, my Lord, kum ba yah, kum ba

yah my Lord, kum ba yah. Kum ba

yah my Lord, kum ba yah. Oh,

Lord, _____ kum ba yah.

2. Someone's crying, Lord, Kum ba yah,

3. Someone's laughing, Lord . . .

4. Someone's singing, Lord . . .

5. Someone's praying, Lord . . .

6. Kum ba yah my Lord . . .

The Beatitudes

Blessed are the poor in spirit:
for theirs is the kingdom of heaven.
Blessed are they that mourn:
for they shall be comforted.
Blessed are the meek:
for they shall inherit the earth.
Blessed are they which do hunger
and thirst after righteousness:
for they shall be filled.

Blessed are the merciful:
  for they shall obtain mercy.
Blessed are the pure in heart:
  for they shall see God.
Blessed are the peace-makers:
  for they shall be called the
  children of God.

Matthew 5:3–9

Prayers

My God, I love you
above all things
because you are all good.
I love you as the creator of life,
I love you as the one
who has forgiven our sins
and opened the gates of heaven.
I love you as the Spirit
whom you have sent among us
to guide us in this world.
Because of my love for you,
I love my neighbor as myself.

                              Amen.

Where Love Is, God Is

by Leo Tolstoy

n a little town in Russia there lived a cobbler, Martin
Avedéaitch by name. He had a tiny room in a basement, the
one window of which looked out on to the street. Through
it one could see only the feet of those who passed by, but
Martin recognized the people by their boots. He had lived long in the
place and had many acquaintances. There was hardly a pair of boots in
the neighborhood that had not been once or twice through his hands,
so he often saw his own handiwork through the window. Some he had
resoled, some patched, some stitched up, and to some he had even put
fresh uppers. He had plenty to do, for he worked well, used good mate-
rial, did not charge too much, and could be relied on. If he could do a
job by the day required, he undertook it; if not, he told the truth and
gave no false promises. So he was well known and never short of work.

Martin had always been a good man, but in his old age he began to

Where Love Is, God Is

think more about his soul and to draw nearer to God. . .

It happened once that Martin sat up late, absorbed in his book. He was reading Luke's Gospel, and in the sixth chapter he came upon the verses:

> To him that smiteth thee on the one cheek offer also the other;
> and from him that taketh away thy cloak withhold not thy coat
> also. Give to every man that asketh thee; and of him that
> taketh away thy goods ask them not again. And as ye would
> that men should do to you, do ye also to them likewise.

He thought about this, and was about to go to bed, but was loath to leave his book. So he went on reading the seventh chapter—about the centurion, the widow's son, and the answer to John's disciples—and he came to the part where a rich Pharisee invited the Lord to his house. And he read how the woman who was a sinner anointed his feet and washed them with her tears, and how he justified her. Coming to the forty-fourth verse, he read:

> And turning to the woman, he said unto Simon, "Seest thou
> this woman? I entered into thine house, thou gavest me no

water for my feet, but she hath wetted my feet with her tears, and wiped them with her hair. Thou gavest me no kiss, but she, since the time I came in, hath not ceased to kiss my feet. My head with oil thou didst not anoint, but she hath anointed my feet with ointment."

He read these verses and thought: "He gave no water for his feet, gave no kiss, his head with oil he did not anoint. . . ." And Martin took off his spectacles once more, laid them on his book, and pondered.

"He must have been like me, that Pharisee. He too thought only of himself—how to get a cup of tea, how to keep warm and comfortable, never a thought of his guest. He took care of himself, but for his guest he cared nothing at all. Yet who was the guest? The Lord himself! If he came to me, should I behave like that?"

Then Martin laid his head upon both his arms and, before he was aware of it, he fell asleep.

"Martin!" He suddenly heard a voice, as if someone had breathed the word above his ear.

He started from his sleep. "Who's there?" he asked.

He turned around and looked at the door; no one was there. He

called again. Then he heard quite distinctly: "Martin, Martin! Look out into the street tomorrow, for I shall come."

Martin roused himself, rose from his chair and rubbed his eyes, but did not know whether he had heard these words in a dream or awake. He put out the lamp and lay down to sleep.

The next morning he rose before daylight, and after saying his prayers he lit the fire and prepared his cabbage soup and buckwheat porridge. Then he lit the samovar, put on his apron, and sat down by the window to his work. . . . Presently an old soldier of Nicholas's reign came near the window, spade in hand. Martin knew him by his boots, which were shabby old felt once, galoshed with leather. The old man was called Stepánitch. A neighboring tradesman kept him in his house for charity, and his duty was to help the house-porter. He began to clear away the snow before Martin's window. Martin glanced at him and then went on with his work.

After he had made a dozen stitches he felt drawn to look out of the window again. He saw that Stepánitch had leaned his spade against the wall, and was either resting himself or trying to get warm. The man was old and broken down, and had evidently not enough strength even to clear away the snow.

Where Love Is, God Is

"What if I called him in and gave him some tea?" thought Martin. "The samovar is just on the boil."

He stuck his awl in its place, and rose, and putting the samovar on the table, made tea. Then he tapped the window with his fingers. Stepánitch turned and came to the window. Martin beckoned to him to come in, and went himself to open the door.

"Come in," he said, "and warm yourself a bit. I'm sure you must be cold."

"May God bless you!" Stepánitch answered. "My bones do ache, to be sure." He came in, first shaking off the snow, and lest he should leave marks on the floor he began wiping his feet. But as did so he tottered and nearly fell.

"Don't trouble to wipe your feet," said Martin. "I'll wipe up the floor—it's all in the day's work. Come, friend, sit down and have some tea."

Filling two tumblers, he passed one to his visitor, and pouring his own tea out into the saucer, began to blow on it.

Stepánitch emptied his glass and, turning it upside down, put the remains of his piece of sugar on the top. He began to express his thanks, but it was plain that he would be glad of some more.

"Have another glass," said Martin, refilling the visitor's tumbler and his own. But while he drank his tea Martin kept looking out into the street.

"Are you expecting anyone?" asked the visitor.

"Am I expecting anyone?" Well, now, I'm ashamed to tell you. It isn't that I really expect anyone, but I heard something last night which I can't get out of my mind. Whether it was a vision, or only a fancy, I can't tell. You see, friend, last night I was reading the Gospel, about Christ the Lord, how he suffered, and how he walked on earth. You have heard tell of it, I dare say."

"I have heard tell of it," answered Stepánitch. "But I'm an ignorant man and not able to read."

"Well, you see, I was reading how he walked on earth. I came to that part, you know, where he went to a Pharisee who did not receive him well. Well, friend, as I read about it, I thought how that man did not receive Christ the Lord with proper honor. Suppose such a thing could happen to such a man as myself, I thought, what would I not do to receive him! But that man gave him no reception at all. Well, friend, as I was thinking of this, I began to doze, and as I dozed I heard some-one call me by name. I got up, and thought I heard someone whispering, 'Expect me. I will come tomorrow.' This happened twice over. And to tell you the truth, it sank so into my mind that, though I am ashamed of it myself, I keep on expecting him, the dear Lord!"

Stepánitch shook his head in silence, finished his tumbler, and laid it on its side, but Martin stood it up again and refilled if for him.

"Thank you, Martin Avedéaitch," he said. "You have given me food and comfort both for soul and body."

"You're very welcome. Come again another time. I am glad to have a guest," said Martin.

Stepánitch went away, and Martin poured out the last of the tea and drank it up. Then he put away the tea things and sat down to his work, stitching the back seam of a boot. And as he stitched he kept looking out of the window and thinking about what he had read in the Bible. And his head was full of Christ's sayings.

Two soldiers went by: one in Government boots, the other in boots of his own; then the master of a neighboring house, in shining galoshes; then a baker carrying a basket. All these passed on. Then a woman came up in worsted stockings and peasant-

made shoes. She passed the window, but stopped by the wall. Martin glanced up at her through the window and saw that she was a stranger, poorly dressed, and with a baby in her arms. She stopped by the wall with her back to the wind, trying to wrap the baby up though she had hardly anything to wrap it in. The woman had only summer clothes on, and even they were shabby and worn. Through the window Martin heard the baby crying, and the woman trying to soothe it, but unable to do so. Martin rose, and going out of the door and up the steps he called to her. "My dear, I say, my dear!"

The woman heard, and turned around.

"Why do you stand out there with the baby in the cold? Come inside. You can wrap him up better in a warm place. Come this way!"

The woman was surprised to see an old man in an apron, with spectacles on his nose, calling to her, but she followed him in.

They went down the steps, entered the little room, and the old man led her to the bed.

"There, sit down, my dear, near the stove. Warm yourself, and feed the baby."

"Haven't any milk. I have eaten nothing myself since early morning," said the woman, but still she took the baby to her breast.

Where Love Is, God Is

Martin shook his head. He brought out a basin and some bread. Then he opened the oven door and poured some cabbage soup into the basin. He took out the porridge pot also, but the porridge was not yet ready, so he spread a cloth on the table and served only the soup and bread.

"Sit down and eat, my dear, and I'll mind the baby. Why, bless me, I've had children of my own; I know how to manage them."

The woman crossed herself, and sitting down at the table began to eat, while Martin put the baby on the bed and sat down by it.

Martin sighed. "Haven't you any warmer clothing?" he asked.

"How could I get warm clothing?" said she. "Why, I pawned my last shawl for sixpence yesterday."

Then the woman came and took the child, and Martin got up. He went and looked among some things that were hanging on the wall, and brought back an old cloak.

"Here," he said, "though it's a worn-out old

thing, it will do to wrap him up in."

The woman looked at the cloak, then at the old man, and taking it, burst into tears. Martin turned away, and groping under the bed brought out a small trunk. He fumbled about in it, and again sat down opposite the woman. And the woman said, "The Lord bless you, friend."

"Take this for Christ's sake," said Martin, and gave her sixpence to get her shawl out of pawn. The woman crossed herself, and Martin did the same, and then he saw her out.

After a while Martin saw an apple-woman stop just in front of his window. On her back she had a sack full of chips, which she was taking home. No doubt she had gathered them at someplace where building was going on.

The sack evidently hurt her, and she wanted to shift it from one shoulder to the other, so she put it down on the footpath and, placing her basket on a post, began to shake down the chips in the sack. While she was doing this, a boy in a tattered cap ran up, snatched an apple out of the basket, and tried to slip away. But the old woman noticed it, and turning, caught the boy by his sleeve. He began to struggle, trying to free himself, but the old woman held on with both hands, knocked

111

his cap off his head, and seized hold of his hair. The boy screamed and the old woman scolded. Martin dropped his awl, not waiting to stick it in its place, and rushed out of the door. Stumbling up the steps and dropping his spectacles in his hurry, he ran out into the street. The old woman was pulling the boy's hair and scolding him, and threatening to take him to the police. The lad was struggling and protesting, saying, "I did not take it. What are you beating me for? Let me go!"

Martin separated them. He took the boy by the hand and said, "Let him go, Granny. Forgive him for Christ's sake."

"I'll pay him out, so that he won't forget it for a year! I'll take the rascal to the police!"

Martin began entreating the old woman.

"Let him go, Granny. He won't do it again."

The old woman let go, and the boy wished to run away, but Martin stopped him. "Ask the Granny's forgiveness!" said he. "And don't do it another time. I saw you take the apple."

The boy began to cry and to beg pardon.

"That's right. And now here's an apple for you," and Martin took an apple from the basket and gave it to the boy, saying, "I will pay you, Granny."

"You will spoil them that way, the young rascals," said the old woman. "He ought to be whipped so that he should remember it for a week."

"Oh, Granny, Granny," said Martin, "that's our way—but it's not God's way. If he should be whipped for stealing an apple, what should be done to us for our sins?"

The old woman was silent. . . .

"God bids us forgive," said Martin, "or else we shall not be forgiven. Forgive everyone, and a thoughtless youngster most of all."

The old woman wagged her head and sighed. . . .

"Of course, it was only his childishness," said she, referring to the boy.

As the old woman was about to hoist her sack on her back, the lad sprang forward to her, saying, "Let me carry it for you, Granny. I'm going that way."

The old woman nodded her head, and put the sack on the boy's back, and they went down the street together, the old woman quite forgetting to ask Martin to pay for the apple. Martin stood and watched them as they went along talking to each other.

When they were out of sight Martin went back to the house. Having found his spectacles unbroken on the steps, he picked up his awl and sat down again to work. He worked a little, but soon could not see to pass the bristle through the holes in the leather, and presently, he noticed the lamplighter passing on his way to light the street lamps.

"Seems it's time to light up," thought he. So he trimmed his lamp, hung it up, and sat down again to work. He finished off one boot and, turning it about, examined it. It was all right. Then he gathered his tools together, swept up the cuttings, put away the bristles and the thread and the awls, and, taking down the lamp, placed it on the table. Then he took the Gospels from the shelf. He meant to open them at the place he had marked the day before with a bit of morocco, but the book opened at another place. As Martin opened it, his yesterday's dream came back to his mind, and no sooner had he thought of it than he seemed to hear footsteps, as though someone were moving behind him. Martin turned round, and it seemed to him as if people were standing in the dark corner, but he could not make out who they were. And a voice whispered in his ear: "Martin, Martin, don't you know me?"

"Who is it?" muttered Martin.

"It is I," said the voice. And out of the dark corner stepped Stepánitch, who smiled and, vanishing like a cloud, was seen no more.

"It is I," said the voice again. And out of the darkness stepped the woman with the baby in her arms, and the woman smiled and the baby laughed, and they too vanished.

"It is I," said the voice once more. And the old woman and the boy with the apple stepped out and both smiled, and then they too vanished.

And Martin's soul grew glad. He crossed himself, put on his spectacles, and began reading the Gospel just where it had opened. And at the top of the page he read:

I was hungry, and ye gave me meat. I was thirsty, and ye gave me drink. I was a stranger, and ye took me in.

And at the bottom of the page he read:

Inasmuch as ye did it unto one of these my brethren, even these least, ye did it unto me.

And Martin understood that his dream had come true, and that the Savior had really come to him that day, and he had welcomed him. ☼

Kind Deeds

by Isaac Watts

Little drops of water,
Little grains of sand.
Make the mighty ocean,
And the pleasant land.

Thus the little minutes,
Humble though they be,
Make the mighty ages
Of eternity.

Little deeds of kindness,
Little words of love,
Make this earth an Eden
Like the heaven above.

The Leaven

A woman woke up early and went to her kitchen to bake bread. She carefully measured out the water, flour, sugar, salt, oil, and most important, the yeast, or leaven. Without yeast, bread wouldn't rise. Bit by bit, the woman stirred the yeast into the water. Round and round she stirred as the birds sang on the windowsill. After the yeast dissolved in the water, she added the other ingredients to make a thick batter. Then she began to knead the batter, like she had done so many times before. Next the woman placed the flat, smooth batter into a pan and put it in the oven. She then went out to the porch to wait.

The birds sang songs to the woman as the aroma of bread floated out from the kitchen. After some time, the woman went inside and opened the oven. Sure enough, the yeast had worked its miracle! The flat, smooth batter had risen into soft, warm bread.

As a little bit of yeast is able to make bread rise, small things can work in big ways.

> *The kingdom of heaven is like yeast that a woman took and mixed into a large amount of flour until it worked all through the dough.*
>
> MATTHEW 13:33

121

The Burning Bush

oses, now a grown man, saw that his people were slaving away harder than ever for the Egyptians. One day, right before his eyes, he saw an Egyptian man kill an Israelite man. In anger, Moses killed the Egyptian man and fled into the desert.

In the desert, Moses met a priest named Jethro. Soon, he married one of Jethro's daughters and began to care for his father-in-law's herd.

One day, Moses decided to lead the sheep and goats across the desert to Sinai, the holy mountain. When he reached the foot of the mountain, he saw before him a bush in flames.

Why doesn't the fire spread, Moses wondered? But the nearby bushes were untouched. He waited for the bush to burn to ash—but that didn't happen either. The fire just kept roaring and raging without doing any harm to the bush.

"Moses! Here I am!" said a voice.

Moses looked about, confused, knowing he was the only person around for miles.

"Do not come any closer," the voice said. "Take off your sandals. You are standing on holy ground."

The voice was coming from the burning bush!

"I am the God of your father, the God of Abraham, the God of Isaac, and the God of Jacob," the voice continued. Moses fell to the ground.

"I have seen how much the Egyptians are making my people

suffer," said the Lord. "So I have come to rescue them. I will bring them out of Egypt, into the beautiful, spacious land that I promised to their fathers. It is a lovely place flowing with milk and honey, a place with plenty of water for crops."

"That is wonderful," Moses said, "but why have you chosen me to tell this to?"

"Because I am sending you to lead my people out of the land of Egypt," God said.

"Why me?" Moses said, nervously. "It's too much for one man to do."

"I will be with you," God reassured him.

"No one will believe that I'm speaking for you," Moses pleaded. "How will I prove that you have sent me?"

"What is that in your hand?" God asked.

"My staff," Moses answered, looking at the long wooden stick.

"Throw it on the ground," God said. Moses did as he was told and the staff promptly turned into a long, hissing snake. Frightened, Moses started to run away but God called him back. "Grab its tail!" the Lord commanded. With trembling hands, Moses reached for the snake, and instantly it became his staff again. "That will be a sign."

"But what if they still don't believe me?" Moses asked.

"Reach into your cloak and then pull your hand out," God said. Moses did as God asked and gasped with disgust when he saw his hand. It was

The Burning Bush

pale and deformed.

"Reach inside again," God said, and again Moses obeyed. When he brought out his hand, it was back to normal. "Now you have two signs."

"But what if they still don't believe me?" Moses said, wanting desperately to find an excuse.

"If they still don't believe you," God said, "you are to pour some river water on the ground. It will turn to blood. That will be the third sign."

"But Lord, you know I'm not a very good speaker," Moses pleaded. "I speak very slowly."

"Am I not the Lord who made your mouth?" God said. "I will teach you what to say."

"Oh, Lord, please, please, please send someone else," Moses begged.

"Fine," God said. "Your brother Aaron shall go with you and I'll be there to help you both. I will tell you what to say, and you will tell Aaron. It will be as if his mouth were yours, and your mouth were mine." Then the fire went out.

Moses returned home, fetched his wife and sons, and they all set off for Egypt, meeting up with Aaron along the way. Moses told Aaron about the burning bush and all that God had said.

At first, the Israelites in Egypt didn't believe that Moses and Aaron had been sent by God. But once they saw God's three signs, they knew it was true. They thanked God for hearing their prayers.

Verses on Love

Love the Lord your God with all your heart and with all your soul and with all your mind and with all your strength. . . . Love your neighbor as yourself. There is no commandment greater than these.

MARK 12:30–31

Dear children, let us not love with words or tongue but with actions and in truth.

1 JOHN 3:18

Do everything in love.

1 CORINTHIANS 16:14

126

Be completely humble and gentle; be patient, bearing with one another in love.

EPHESIANS 4:2

If I speak in the tongues of men and of angels, but have not love, I am only a resounding gong or a clanging cymbal.

If I have the gift of prophecy and can fathom all mysteries and all knowledge, and if I have a faith that can move mountains, but have not love, I am nothing.

If I give all I possess to the poor and surrender my body to the flames, but have not love, I gain nothing.

Love is patient, love is kind. It does not envy, it does not boast, it is not proud.

It is not rude, it is not self-seeking, it is not easily angered, it keeps no record of wrongs.

Love does not delight in evil but rejoices with the truth. It always protects, always trusts, always hopes, always perseveres.

Love never fails. But where there are prophecies, they will cease; where there are tongues, they will be stilled; where there is knowledge, it will pass away. . . .

And now these three remain: faith, hope and love. But the greatest of these is love.

1 CORINTHIANS 13:1–8, 13

Jesus Loves Me

Je - sus loves me, this I know, for the Bi - ble tells me so;

Lit - tle ones to Him be - long, They are weak, but He is strong.

Yes, Je - sus loves me, Yes, Je - sus loves me,

Yes, Je - sus loves me, The Bi - ble tells me so.

132

Prayers

Father, help each little child,
Make us truthful, good, and mild,
Kind, obedient, modest, meek,
Mindful of the words we speak.

What is right may we pursue,
What is wrong refuse to do.
What is evil seek to shun,
This we ask for everyone.

Amen.

Crossing the Red Sea

ne day, God warned Moses and Aaron that he was going to bring judgment against Pharaoh and the Egyptians for bringing trouble upon the Israelites. This judgment would be in the form of ten plagues as well as the slaying of every first-born child and animal.

Moses and Aaron were told by God to tell each Israelite family to slaughter a lamb and smear its blood on their front door. God "passed over" every home that had its front door covered in blood.

Fearing God's further wrath, Pharaoh commanded the Israelites to leave Egypt immediately. Moses and Aaron gathered everyone together.

Moses pointed to the only cloud in the sky.

"We shall follow that cloud," he said. "God is up there leading us. At night, it will become a cloud of fire to help us see in the darkness. That way we'll always know where to go."

The people started off along the desert road; Moses, his family, and Aaron up front, and the rest of the Israelites behind. They spread out across the entire road and extended back for many miles. The Israelites brought all their belongings, including their herds of cattle, sheep, and goats.

The Israelites walked and walked, following the cloud by day and the firelight by night. If anyone stopped to rest it was never for long. Finally, they reached the Red Sea.

Meanwhile, back in Egypt, Pharaoh

decided he needed his slaves. "Who will make the bricks? Who will build for us?" He quickly rounded up his army troops and six hundred chariots and horsemen. "Follow the Israelites!" he commanded. The Egyptians set off.

On the shores of the Red Sea, God spoke to Moses. "Make your camp here," he said. "When Pharaoh finds out where you are, he'll think he has you trapped between the water and his army. But he'll be wrong. I'll perform a miracle to set you free, and the Egyptians will then know that I am the mighty Lord."

Moses told the Israelites the plan, and they set up camp on the shore of the Red Sea. They put up tents, took off their shoes, cooked meals over small fires, and fed the cattle, sheep, and goats. Just as they were settling in, they felt the ground shaking.

"The Egyptians are coming! The Egyptians are coming!" cried a young boy on the outskirts of the camp.

Everyone jumped up in fear, not knowing which way to go. If they went back the way they came, they'd surely be killed by the Egyptians. But if they went in the direction of the sea, they'd surely drown!

135

"We're trapped!" cried a woman. "Pharaoh's army has hunted us down!"

They could make out a huge cloud of dust coming their way. As it came closer, they could see horses, chariot wheels, and men.

"What have you done to us, Moses?" the Israelites cried. "Did you bring us out of Egypt just so we could be killed in the desert?"

"We would rather have remained slaves. At least then we'd stay alive!"

Moses did his best to calm his people. "It only looks like we're trapped!" he answered. "God will help us escape! He's on our side!" But no one believed him. The adults tried to think up plans to cross the sea, but one plan sounded more ridiculous than the next. People ran around in fear and children cried. Everything was in total chaos.

Meanwhile, the chariots were coming closer and closer. Soon the entire army would be on top of them!

"Don't be afraid!" Moses cried. "Be patient and trust God!" But the Israelites were too frightened to listen to him.

"Why are you crying out like

that?" God said to Moses.

"I have to," Moses said, relieved to hear God's voice. "How else can I get them to calm down?"

"Raise your arm and stretch it over the sea," God instructed. "The sea will split into two parts, making a dry path in between for you to walk on."

Moses did as the Lord said and the sea split into two parts!

"Follow me!" Moses said, and he led the Israelites down a long, dry path between two tall walls of waves. "God will protect us."

Everyone walked in awed silence.

No one could believe they were actually walking across the Red Sea! But they were—and they knew it was God's work.

Just as Moses reached the opposite shore, the Egyptians reached the Red Sea and saw the strange dry path running through it. They were every bit as stunned as the Israelites but that didn't stop them from following the Israelites. The Egyptian army followed the Israelites along the dry path between the two walls of waves in the middle of the sea.

"We made it!" Israelites started to

yell as they reached the opposite shore.

"God has saved us!"

"We're free at last!"

"Not quite!" cried the last man to reach the shore. "Pharaoh's army is following us!"

Everyone turned back toward the sea and saw the Egyptian army troops and the hundreds of horsemen and chariots racing between the walls of waves.

"Stretch your arm over the sea," God said to Moses. "But this time do it in the opposite direction."

Moses did as he was told and, suddenly, a strong wind blew and the walls of waves came crashing down into the sea. Every trace of the path was gone, and all the chariots, horsemen, and army troops were swept away by the sea. At last the Israelites were free.

Now that the Israelites knew how powerful their Lord was they felt happy, safe, and loved. They'd always remember how he led them on a dry land through the sea.

Onward, Christian Soldiers

On-ward Chris-tian sol - diers, March-ing as to war,

With the cross of Je - sus Go-ing on be - fore!

Christ the Roy - al Mas - ter, Leads a - gainst the foe;

For-ward in - to bat - tle, __ See His ban-ners go.

On-ward Chris-tian sol - diers, __ March-ing as to __ war,

with the cross of Je - sus Go - ing on be - fore.

He Will Hear

by Jane Taylor

God is so good that he will hear
Whenever children humbly pray.
He always lends a gracious ear
To what the youngest child may say.

His own most holy Book declares
He loves good little children still,
And that he listens to their prayers
Just as a tender father will.

*Bless us, O Lord, and these your gifts,
which we are about to receive from your
goodness, through Christ our Lord.*
Amen.

The Frogs and Their King

In the days of old, the frogs met to beg God to send them a king. So he threw them a log and said, "There's a king for you—a good, mild one!"

Well, King Log landed on the pond with such a splash that the frogs scattered off in fright. Some sought the mud, and some the reeds. For a long time, not a single frog in the pond would dare make a peep.

By and by, when they saw that King Log lay quiet and still, they said, "See, he sleeps!" Some hopped around him, nearer and nearer, 'til, one by one, they leapt on his back. Finally, when nothing they did made King Log stir, the frogs grew angry. So, with harsh croaks, they begged God to give them a king with more life.

God then sent them an eel. But the frogs soon found that he, too, was too tame for them. So, they asked God a third time for a king with more strength of will. This time, God sent them a stork. The new king, day by day, made the frogs his prey, 'til there were none left to croak on the lake, except one. The last frog shook his head and said, "If we had only had the sense to keep well, and be happy with what we had."

Trust in God's wisdom and be thankful of his gifts.

Do not be anxious about anything, but in everything, by prayer and petition, with thanksgiving, present your requests to God.

PHILIPPIANS 4:6

Verses on Prayer

The Lord is near to all who call on him, to all who call on him in truth.

PSALM 145:18

Pray continually.

1 THESSALONIANS 5:17

Is any one of you in trouble? He should pray. Is anyone happy? Let him sing songs of praise.

JAMES 5:13

And the prayer offered in faith will make the sick person well; the Lord will raise him up. If he has sinned, he will be forgiven.

JAMES 5:15

149

The Ten Commandments

or many weeks, Moses led the men, women, and children of Israel through the desert. The sun scorched the sand and the sand scorched their feet. And there was hardly any food or water. The people of Israel were very hungry and thirsty.

One day they came to a pool of water.

"Hurray!" yelled everyone, rushing toward the pool with jugs, buckets, and cupped hands. But the pool smelled horrible—the water was sour!

"We'd be better off as slaves in Egypt!" one man yelled to Moses.

"At least as slaves we had water, fresh fruit, and fish!" moaned a woman.

"Why have you led us away to starve to death?" cried someone else.

Moses called out to God, and the Lord pointed out a piece of wood and told him to throw it into the pool. Moses did as he was told and the water became sweet and fresh.

The people of Israel filled their buckets, jugs, and cupped hands. They drank and drank, then they rested and drank some more.

"Always remember," Moses told them, "God is watching over us."

It was true! For the next morning when they woke up, the ground was covered with tiny dewdrops. When the sun dried the dew, it turned into breadcrumbs—and no one likes breadcrumbs more than birds.

When a flock of birds came to feast, the people caught as many of them as they needed, cooked them over their fires, and ate. From that day on, God made sure they had food and water.

Finally, after three long months, the people of Israel arrived at Mount Sinai. "At last!" they cried, and then went about setting up camp near the foot of the giant mountain.

"It feels so good to rest my feet!" said a woman.

"It feels so good to put down our parcels!" said two children.

"It feels so good to..." said a man. He meant to say "sleep" but he couldn't stay awake long enough!

For two days, the people of Israel spent most of their time relaxing. Their legs and arms ached from walking, their backs were tired from carrying things, and their eyes were tired from squinting in the sun. When they weren't resting, the women cooked, the men cared for the animals, and the children played. Whenever the children saw Moses, they followed at his heels. He was their favorite of all the grown-ups.

On the morning of the third day, the mountain began to tremble.

The Ten Commandments

Lightning flashed, thunder crashed—boom! The top of the mountain disappeared in a thick, gray cloud. Suddenly, the sound of a trumpet filled the air. Moses recognized it as a sign. God was calling to him to bring the people of Israel to the foot of the mountain.

Moses quickly gathered the people at the foot of the mountain where the sound of the trumpet got louder and louder. Finally it stopped, and God spoke these words: "I am the Lord your God, who brought you out of Egypt, out of the land of slavery.

"You shall worship no other gods but me.

"You shall not make statues to worship.

"You shall not misuse my name—only use my name when praying.

"Do not work on the seventh day of the week. It's the Sabbath, and you shall do nothing but rest.

"Listen to your father and mother, and respect them.

"You shall not kill another person.

"You shall not take a man or woman away from his wife or her husband.

"You shall not steal something that doesn't belong to you.

152

The Ten Commandments

"You shall not make things up about yourself or someone else.

"You shall not wish for things you do not have."

When God finished speaking, another loud trumpet sounded, and then there was a moment of silence. Moses noticed that most people were trembling with fear.

"Don't be afraid of God," Moses said to them. "We are his people and he has given us ten laws, or commandments, to live by. The commandments will show us how to love God and each other. If we follow them, we shall live a very good life." The people listened, still afraid.

Then God spoke to Moses again. "Come up to me," he said. "I have something to give you."

The people watched as Moses began to climb the mountain and disappear into the thick, gray cloud. Minutes passed. Hours passed. Days passed. A week passed. And there was still no sign of Moses. The people returned to their camp to wait. Two weeks passed. A month passed. And still no sign of Moses.

Will Moses ever return, the people of Israel wondered?

Finally, after spending forty days and forty nights at the top of the mountain, Moses returned. He carried with him two tablets of stone with the Ten Commandments written on them. It was God's gift to the people. Now they would always remember how to live their lives.

The Ten Commandments

You shall have no
other gods before me.

You shall not make for
yourself an idol.

You shall not misuse
the name of the
Lord your God.

Remember the Sabbath
day by keeping it holy.

Honor your father
and your mother.

You shall not murder.

You shall not
commit adultery.

You shall not steal.

You shall not give false
testimony against
your neighbor.

You shall not covet
anything that belongs
to your neighbor.

Saturday Night

Haste, put your playthings all away,
Tomorrow is the Sabbath day;
Come, bring to me your Noah's ark,
Put by your pretty music cart;
Because, my love, you must not play,
But holy keep the Sabbath day.

Bring me your German village, please,
With all its houses, gates, and trees;
Your waxen doll with eyes so blue,
And all her tea things, bright and new;
Because, you know, you must not play,
But love to keep the Sabbath day.

Now take your Sunday pictures down—
King David with his harp and crown,
Good little Samuel on his knees,
And many pleasant sights like these;
Because, you know, you must not play,
But learn of God upon his day.

There is your hymn-book—you shall learn
A verse, and some sweet kisses earn;
Your book of Bible stories, too,
Which dear mamma will read to you;
I think, that though you must not play,
We'll have a happy Sabbath day.

S. Prout Newcombe, Pleasant Pages for Young People, 1879

Obey Your Parents

The New Class Books for Sabbath Schools: Second Reading Lessons, c. 1875

ext to the fear and love of God who made you, it is your duty to honour and obey your father and mother. This is the command of the Lord in His own word; and it is very right. . . .

For who, when you were a little helpless baby, watched over you, and kept you from harm? Who fed you and clothed you, and was always ready to help you when you could not help yourself?

Did not your father and mother do all this, and more than this for you? . . . the Lord is very good to those who love their parents, as He said in the promise, 'Honour thy father and mother, that thy days may be long in the land which the Lord thy God giveth thee.'

Our Lord Jesus also, when he was a child, was subject unto his parents, and thus he grew 'in wisdom and stature, and in favour with God and man.' Try to be like Him.

If you thus love and honour your father and mother, you will grow up to be wise and happy.

The B-I-B-L-E

The B - I - B - L - E, yes,

that's the book for me, I stand a - lone on the

Word of God, The B - I - B - L - E.

Little Sunshine

Retold by Etta Austin Blaisdell
and Mary Frances Blaisdell

nce there was a little girl named Elsa. She had a very old grandmother, with white hair, and wrinkles all over her face. Elsa's father had a large house that stood on a hill.

Each day the sun peeped in at the south windows. It made everything look bright and beautiful.

The grandmother lived on the north side of the house. The sun never came to her room.

One day Elsa said to her father, "Why doesn't the sun peep into Grandma's room? I know she would like to have him."

"The sun cannot look in at the north windows," said her father.

"Then let us turn the house around, Papa."

"It is much too large for that," said her father.

"Will Grandma never have any sunshine in her room?" asked Elsa.

Little Sunshine

"Of course not, my child, unless you can carry some to her."

After that Elsa tried and tried to think how she could carry the sunshine to her grandmother.

When she played in the fields she saw the grass and the flowers nodding their heads. The birds sang sweetly as they flew from tree to tree.

Everything seemed to say, "We love the sun. We love the bright, warm sun."

"Grandma would love it, too," thought the child. "I must take some to her."

When she was in the garden one morning she felt the sun's warm rays in her golden hair. Then she sat down and she saw them in her lap.

"I will take them in my dress," she thought, "and carry them to Grandma's room." So she jumped up and ran into the house.

"Look, Grandma, look! I have some sunshine for you," she cried. And she opened her dress, but there was not a ray to be seen.

163

Little Sunshine

"It peeps out of your eyes, my child," said her grandmother, "and it shines in your sunny, golden hair. I do not need the sun when I have you with me."

Elsa did not understand how the sun could peep out of her eyes. But she was glad to make her dear grandmother happy.

Every morning she played in the garden. Then she ran to her grandmother's room to carry the sunshine in her eyes and hair.

This is the day which
the Lord has made;
let us rejoice and
be glad in it.

PSALM 118:24

The Lark and the Finch

poor lark was kept in a cage that hung on a wall in an old village that was full of dust and dirt. Every morning, the lark would rest on his perch and sing the sweetest song. One day, a finch happened to fly near the open window and hear the lark's song.

"O, poor lark!" cried the finch from the windowsill. "You live in such a dreary little house in this dirty town. Yet your song is the most beautiful thing in the village. How is it possible that you can sing so joyful a melody while you are locked up in a terrible cage?"

"Finch, finch," rang out the lark, in his clear and lovely tones, "Why should my spirit remained caged simply because I am? Don't you know that if I didn't sing while I'm shut up here, I might fail to remember my song when the time comes for me to be free and fly up into the sky?"

It is meant for us to sing hymns of praise while we are on earth so we will be prepared for our flight to heaven.

Give Me Oil in My Lamp

Give me oil in my lamp, Keep me burn-ing, ___ Give me

oil in my lamp, I pray, Give me

oil in my lamp, Keep me burn - ing, ___ Keep me

burn - ing 'til the break of day.

Sing "Ho - san na", sing "Ho - san - na",

sing "Ho - san - na to the King of Kings".

Sing "Ho - san - na", sing "Ho - san - na",

Sing "Ho - san - na to the King".

2. Give me joy in my heart, keep me praising.
   Give me joy in my heart, I pray.
   Give me joy in my heart, keep me praising
   Keep me praising Him till break of day.

Refrain

3. Give me love in my heart, keep me serving.
   Give me love in my heart, I pray.
   Give me love in my heart, keep me serving.
   Keep me serving Him till break of day.

Refrain

Let Us Make a Joyful Noise

Let them praise

his name with

dancing and make

music to him

with tambourine

and harp.

PSALM 149:3

Children love making music. Form a band! Create instruments together and decorate with construction paper and markers. Then, sing songs of praise.

Shakers
dried beans or rice, small tin cans, masking tape
1. Fill cans about half full with dried beans or rice.
2. Cover with plastic lid, if available, or tape.
3. Experiment for different sounds and rhythms. Hold the shaker sideways and tip it slowly so the beans slide from one end to the other. Or shake it quickly up and down for a loud rattle.

Tambourines
2 heavy-duty paper plates, a handful of dried corn or peas, masking tape
1. Place the dried corn or peas on one plate. Cover it with the other plate.
2. Tape the edges together to form a tight seal.
3. Hold your tambourine with one hand and tap it with the other. How many ways can you vary the sound? Use your palm or fingertips or try slapping it against your leg.

Box Harp
shoebox with lid, large rubber bands, pencil, 3 x ½-inch rubber eraser
1. Stretch the rubber bands around the box.
2. Slide the pencil under the rubber bands to create a bridge. Wedge the eraser underneath one end of the pencil. Pluck.
Variation: To make a Box Zither, cut a hole in the lid of the shoebox before stretching the rubber bands across. Slide a pencil under the rubber bands on either side of the hole.

On Song and Praise

The Lord is my strength and my song; he has become my salvation. He is my God, and I will praise him, my father's God, and I will exalt him.

EXODUS 15:2

Sing to him, sing praise to him; tell of all his wonderful acts.

1 CHRONICLES 16:9

Let the sea resound, and all that is in it; let the fields be jubilant, and everything in them! Then the trees of the forest will sing, they will sing for joy before the Lord, for he comes to judge the earth.

1 CHRONICLES 16:32–33

The Lord is my strength and my shield;
my heart trusts in him, and I am helped.
My heart leaps for joy and I will give
thanks to him in song.

PSALM 28:7

Praised Be My Lord
by St. Francis of Assisi

Praisèd be my Lord God for all his creatures,
and especially our brother the sun, who
brings us the day and brings us the light;
fair is he and shines with a great splendour;
O Lord, he signifies to us thee.

Praisèd be my Lord for our sister the moon,
and for the stars, which he has set clear
and lovely in the heaven.

Praisèd by my Lord for our brother the wind,
and for air and cloud, calms and all weather,
by which thou upholdest life in all creatures.

Prayers

Praisèd be my Lord for our sister water, who is very serviceable unto us and humble and precious and clean.

Praisèd be my Lord for our brother fire, through whom thou givest light in the darkness; and he is bright and pleasant and very mighty and strong.

Praisèd be my Lord for our mother the earth, who doth sustain and keep us, and bringest forth divers fruits and flowers of many colors, and grass.

Praise ye and bless ye the Lord, and give thanks unto him, and serve him with great humility.

Amen.

Fall of Jericho

oses died, and a man named Joshua took his place as leader of the people of Israel, now known as God's people. After forty years of wandering, they finally reached the Jordan River. Across the river was the land God had promised them.

"Before we can settle there we must defeat our enemies who live there," Joshua explained. "We must capture the city of Jericho."

No one was looking forward to a battle—but if they had to fight to get the land God promised them, then that's what they would do.

The people of Israel set up camp along the riverbank. From there, they could see the high, stone wall that circled the city of Jericho. They never saw anyone go in, they never saw anyone go out. All they saw were guards stationed along the top of the wall.

Joshua called two of his bravest, strongest men to his side. "Sneak into Jericho," he told them. "Spy on the people and see if the people are ready to fight us. Find out how strong their army is. Then come back and tell me what you have learned. We must know more about our enemies before we attack."

The two spies set off at once. When they arrived at the wall, they sneaked through a heavy, iron gate as quietly as they could—but it wasn't quiet enough!

"Stop where you are!" shouted a voice. As heavy footsteps headed toward them, the spies raced down an unfamiliar winding street. The footsteps followed them as they turned into a dead-end alley. They were trapped!

"Quick! In here!" a voice whispered from an open window. "Don't worry. You'll be safe."

Having no other choice, the spies climbed in through a window and found themselves in a small room with a beautiful woman.

"My name is Rahab," said the woman. "You can hide upstairs." She led the men upstairs and looked at them closely. "You're the people of Israel, aren't you?" The spies nodded, wondering if Rahab could be trusted. "I know all about your people," Rahab said. "God blesses whatever

you do. That's why the men in Jericho are scared to fight you."

"They are?" said one of the spies. Joshua would be happy to hear that!

Rahab nodded. "If I help you escape, will you see that my family stays safe when your people take Jericho?"

"Yes," said the other spy. "But only if we don't get caught."

"That's fair," Rahab said. Then she showed them a secret staircase that led to a window that led to a place outside the city walls. She handed them a piece of long, red rope to climb down.

"Hang this red rope out your window when we attack Jericho," said one of the spies. "We'll tell our soldiers to leave the house with the red rope alone." Rahab nodded

Fall of Jericho

gratefully, and the two spies escaped.

When they returned to Joshua and told him the good news, Joshua prayed to God, and God answered by giving him a strange plan. Joshua told the plan to his soldiers.

"Instead of a battle," Joshua said, "we will have a parade."

"A parade?" said the soldiers, wondering if they had heard right. But Joshua just nodded and continued describing the parade. When he finished, the soldiers said, "If God wants us to have a parade, we will have a parade."

And so they lined up and marched over to the wall surrounding Jericho.

First came seven priests carrying a wooden ark that held the symbol of God and blowing trumpets.

Next came Joshua, the leader of his people.

Next came hundreds and hundreds of soldiers.

When the guards saw them, they trembled with fear. "The battle will soon begin," they said. "We will all die because God is on their side," they warned the soldiers on the other side of the wall.

But the people of Israel surprised them. Instead of attacking, they paraded peacefully around the walls surrounding the city. There were no shouts or yells or battle cries—only the sound of trumpets. After they went around once, they returned to their camp and rested.

They did the same thing the next day, and the next, and the next, and

Fall of Jericho

the next. For six days, they proudly paraded around the city of Jericho. The only sounds came from the priests' trumpets.

On the seventh day, the priests and Joshua's army marched around the city one . . . two . . . three . . . four . . . five . . . six . . . seven times! Then the soldiers let out a whoop.

CRASH! BOOM!

Within seconds of the last trumpet sound, the walls of Jericho crumbled to the ground. God had made a miracle! The soldiers of Israel—God's soldiers—climbed over the loose stone, poured into the city, and took Jericho for their own. The only house they left alone was the one with the red rope hanging from the window. Rahab and her family were safe and lived among God's people for many years.

181

The Saints Go Marching In

I am just a lone - ly trav -'ler, _____ through this

big, wide world of sin; Want to

join that grand pro - cess - ion, _____ when the

saints go march - ing in. _____ Oh, when the

184

saints _____ go march - ing in, _____ Oh when the

saints go march - ing in, Oh I

want to be in their num - ber ____ When the

saints go march - ing in. _____

We Thank Thee

by Ralph Waldo Emerson

For flowers that bloom about our feet;
For tender grass so fresh and sweet;
For song of bird and hum of bee;
For all things fair we hear or see—
　　　Father in Heaven, we thank Thee!

For blue of stream, and blue of sky;
For pleasant shade of branches high;
For fragrant air and cooling breeze;
For beauty of the blooming trees—
　　　Father in Heaven, we thank Thee!

Prayers

For mother-love, for father-care;
For brothers strong and sisters fair;
For love at home and school each day;
For guidance lest we go astray—
    Father in Heaven, we thank Thee!

For Thy dear, everlasting arms,
That bear us o'er all ills and harms;
For blessed words of long ago,
That help us now Thy will to know—
    Father in Heaven, we thank Thee!

The Sower of Seeds

A farmer went out to sow his seed. As he was scattering the seed, some fell along the path and the birds came and ate it up. Some seed fell on a shallow layer of soil that lay on top of rocky ground. They sprouted quickly into tall green plants—but when the sun came out they dried out and died just as quickly. You see, the plants hadn't been able to grow roots in the rocky ground, which had no moisture.

Some seed fell among thorns, which grew very fast. Though the plants grew tall, the thorns grew even taller and eventually choked the plants before they could mature.

And some seed fell on good, rich soil, where it grew…and grew… and grew until it covered many acres of land! Though only a few of the farmer's seeds landed on good, rich soil, they produced a crop a hundred times larger than all that was sown.

The seed is like the word of God. The chosen few who open their hearts and understand will grow vibrantly, blossoming as God's children.

> *Still other seed fell on good soil, where it produced a crop.*
> MATTHEW 13:8

189

Gardening God's Way

Plant three rows of peas:
Peace of mind
Peace of heart
Peace of soul

Plant four rows of squash:
Squash gossip
Squash indifference
Squash grumbling
Squash selfishness

Plant four rows of lettuce:
Lettuce be faithful
Lettuce be kind
Lettuce be obedient
Lettuce really love one another

No garden without turnips:
Turnip for meetings
Turnip for service
Turnip to help one another

Water freely with patience and
Cultivate with love.
There is much fruit in your garden
Because you reap what you sow.

To conclude our garden
We must have thyme:
Thyme for God
Thyme for study
Thyme for prayer

Naomi and Ruth

n the land of Moab there lived a man named Elimelech, his wife Naomi, and their two sons. Most of the people in Moab worshiped a false god—but not this family. Elimelech and Naomi worshiped the one true God, and they taught their sons to do the same.

One day Elimelech died leaving his two sons to take care of their mother, Naomi. The boys were happy to do this for they loved their mother very much.

When the sons grew older, they each married a young woman from Moab. Though the people of Moab and the people of Israel had been enemies for many years, Naomi welcomed the two young women into their home with open arms. She taught them about the one true God, and she loved them as if they were her own daughters.

For the next few years, they lived comfortably. Naomi's sons worked in the fields while she and her sons' wives, Orpah and Ruth, worked at home, talking and laughing as they washed clothes, cleaned house, and cooked tasty meals.

Then suddenly the two sons died, leaving Naomi and her daughters-in-law alone.

The sons couldn't have died at a worse time, for it hadn't rained for months and food was very scarce. Orpah and Ruth went to work in the fields, but there was little grain to be found. If the three of them stayed in Moab they would surely starve.

"My daughters," Naomi said one morning, "I'm going to return to Bethlehem, the land where I grew up. I've heard there is plenty of food there, and I can see my people again. It would be best for you to go back to your own parents. They will take good care of you and make sure you have plenty to eat."

"I want to go with you!" Ruth said, for she'd grown to love Naomi very much.

"I do, too!" Orpah said.

"No," Naomi said, shaking her head. "I'm a burden to you. Go find yourselves new husbands."

"You're not a burden to us at all," Ruth said.

Orpah, after much hesitation, said, "I will do as you wish. But I will always miss you." She threw her arms around Naomi and the two women cried for a long time. Bethlehem was very far away from Moab and they knew they'd never see each other again.

"Go, Ruth," Naomi said after Orpah left. But Ruth refused.

"I will stay with you no matter what happens," Ruth said stubbornly. "Wherever you go I will go. You're my mother now. Your people will be my people, and your God will be my God. God will take care of us."

"That he will," Naomi said, realizing she'd never convince Ruth to leave her. Anyway she was happy to have Ruth's company. So the two of them set off to Bethlehem.

"You've come back to us!" Naomi's

194

Naomi and Ruth

friends and relatives said when they saw her. They hugged her warmly, and looked curiously at the lovely young woman at her side.

"This is my daughter-in-law Ruth," Naomi said. "I don't know what I would do without her." Then she told them the sad news about her husband and sons.

Ruth was amazed at how loving and generous Naomi's family was. The relatives helped them find a small shelter and gave them some firewood and food.

"The harvest has started," Ruth said to Naomi one day. "I'm going to go into the fields to collect left-over barley. I'll bring home whatever I find."

"I wish I could go with you," Naomi said, "but I am old and . . . ."

"You've taken great care of me ever since I married your son, and now it's my turn to take care of you," Ruth replied.

The next morning, Ruth carried a great basket to a field owned by a rich cousin of Naomi named Boaz. Boaz had heard Naomi was back, but he hadn't seen her yet. When Boaz saw the lovely young woman coming up his path he went out to meet her.

"Can I help you?" he asked kindly.

"Please, sir," Ruth said, "may I collect the leftover barley that your servants leave behind? My mother-in-

law and I need to eat."

"What's mine is yours," Boaz said, gesturing toward his fields.

Grateful for Boaz's kindness, Ruth went out to the field and began to collect barley. By the time darkness fell, she had filled the entire basket.

"Where on earth did you find so much food?" Naomi asked when Ruth returned. "It will last us a week!"

"Oh, Naomi!" Ruth said, her face flushed. "I met the nicest man. His name is Boaz and he said what's his is mine."

Naomi said "Boaz is my relative! If Boaz is helping us God must be looking out for us."

Naomi was right—God was looking out for them. For the rest of the harvest Ruth worked in Boaz's field, and there was always more than enough food on their table.

Meanwhile, Ruth and Boaz were growing to be quite fond of each other. At the end of the harvest, they decided to get married. Soon after, God blessed them with a little boy named Obed. No one was happier than Naomi, who moved in with Boaz and Ruth to take care of her new little grandson. When Obed grew up, he had a son called Jesse, who had a son named David, the shepherd boy who became the King of Israel. ✳

Garden Song

Words and Music by Dave Mallett

Inch by inch, row by __ row, __ gon - na make this
gar - den grow __ All it takes is a rake and a hoe and a
piece of fer - tile ground. __ Inch by inch, row by __ row, __
Some - one bless __ the seeds I sow, __ Some - one warm them
from be - low __ 'til the rain comes tum - bl - ing down.

Pull-ing weeds_ and pick-in' stones_ man is made_ of dreams
_ and bones_ Feel the need to grow my own _ 'cause the
time is ___close at hand. _ Grain for grain, sun and _rain, _
Find my way in na-ture's chain, _ To my bod-y
and my brain, to the mu-sic from the land. ___
Plant your rows _ straight and long, _ thick-er than _ with

Garden Song (continued)

pray'r and song,   Moth-er Earth will   make you strong if you

give her   love and   care.   Old __ crow watch-in'

hun - gri - ly __   from his perch __   in   yon - der   tree,

In my gar-den   I'm as free _ as that feath-ered beak up there.

Inch   by   inch,   row by __ row, __   gon-na make this gar-den grow, __ All it takes is a rake and a hoe and a

piece of fer - tile ground. ___ Inch by inch,

row by row, __ some-one bless the seeds I sow,

Some - one warm ___ them from be - low ___ 'til the

rain comes tum - bl - ing down.

*O God, make us children
of quietness and heirs
of peace. Amen.*

St. Clement

Growing Plants & Flowers

... whoever sows

generously will also

reap generously.

2 CORINTHIANS 9:6

Jesus said even faith as small as a mustard seed can move mountains. Show your children what a little seed or bulb can become. Plant mustard! Radishes also sprout quickly and are easy to grow. Or bring nature inside with a bit of indoor gardening.

Seeds of Faith
egg carton, soil, mustard seeds

1. Fill each egg compartment with soil.
2. Poke a 1/4-inch hole in each pocket of soil. Drop in 2 or 3 seeds and cover.
3. Water, keeping the soil evenly moist. Seeds will sprout within a week.

Sow a Garden
radish seeds, garden plot

1. In early spring, turn over a row of dirt.
2. With a stick, dig a trench about 1/4-inch deep.
3. Sprinkle seeds into trench and cover with dirt.
4. When sprouts are 2 inches high (about 1 1/2 weeks), thin out seedlings. Give sprouts at least an inch of growing room on either side.
5. Radishes will be ready to eat in three to four weeks.

Force Bulbs
large glass saucer or pie plate, gravel, bulbs (tulip, daffodil, or narcissus)

1. Place bulbs in saucer and cover them with gravel. Be sure to leave the bulb tips slightly exposed.
2. Fill the bottom of the saucer with water.
3. Store in a cool, dark closet or cupboard.
4. Maintain water level and watch as roots and shoots grow.
5. In about six weeks, bring your bulbs into the daylight and watch them bloom.

The Field of Corn

An old man had a field. One day, he fell ill and sent for his three sons. He wanted to say farewell and give them one last instruction.

"My sons," said he, "there is one thing I want you to do. Find the rich gift that I have left for you in my field . . . ." Here the poor old man's voice grew faint, and he took his last breath.

The sons were too sad to follow their father's wishes. But in time, their want drove them to seek for what they thought must be buried gold. So, they dug up the field until there was not a rock unturned.

At last they gave it up.

"It's strange that our old father should have us look so long and hard for something that isn't here," said Jack.

"Come," said Dick, "since we have turned all the soil in the field, we may as well sow it with corn and make the most of it."

The brothers set to work. In due time, a crop sprang up five times as large as the crops that had grown there in their father's time. The thought struck them that their father had hoped they would earn their bread by the sweat of their brow.

Seek 'til you find, and your work will be rewarded.

Trees

by Joyce Kilmer

I think that I shall never see
A poem lovely as a tree.

A tree whose hungry mouth is pressed
Against the earth's sweet flowing breast;

A tree that looks at God all day
And lifts her leafy arms to pray;

A tree that may in summer wear
A nest of robins in her hair;

Upon whose bosom snow has lain;
Who intimately lives with rain.

Poems are made by fools like me,
But only God can make a tree.

David and Goliath

here was once a very greedy king named Saul. God was so disappointed with King Saul's selfish ways that he chose a young shepherd named David to replace him when the time came. David, the youngest of eight brothers, had a warm smile and a generous heart.

While David tended sheep in the pasture, God often spoke to him. Whether he was chasing away wolves with his slingshot, playing his harp and singing, or having lunch under a tree, David always stopped what he was doing to listen. And as David grew older, he felt himself growing closer and closer to God.

At the time, many battles were being fought between the Israelites and the Philistines. David always knew about them because three of his brothers were King Saul's soldiers. His father, Jesse, often asked David to bring his brothers bread and cheese. That way, he could find out how his sons were doing.

One day, when David brought food to his brothers in their camp in the Valley of Elah, he found them huddled together with the other Israelite soldiers. They were talking about a new Philistine soldier from Gath named Goliath.

"I'm not fighting with Goliath on the other side!" said the bravest soldier.

"Me neither," said the strongest soldier. "He's not going to stick me with that three-hundred-pound

bronze sword or that five-hundred-pound iron spear."

"Did you see the size of him?" exclaimed David's tallest brother. "I wouldn't get in his way for all the silver in the world!"

"King Saul says we must fight," said David's smartest brother. "But what good would that do us? We have no chance of winning."

David couldn't believe his ears! He had never heard his brothers or the other Israelite soldiers talk this way. Usually they were brave, strong, and confident.

THUMP, THUMP, THUMP, THUMP. Heavy footsteps rumbled and shook the ground as they approached the Israelite camp. When David saw who it was he couldn't believe his eyes. There in front of them was the biggest, strongest, ugliest, meanest man he had ever seen. Not a man—a giant!

"CHOOSE A MAN TO FIGHT ME!" Goliath said in a loud, booming voice. "IF HE WINS THE FIGHT AND KILLS ME, WE WILL BECOME YOUR SLAVES. BUT IF I WIN THE FIGHT AND KILL HIM, YOU WILL BECOME OUR SLAVES."

Though it was difficult to do, David tore his eyes away from the giant to see how the Israelite soldiers would respond. They were all trembling with fear, including King Saul, who had just arrived. When he saw the giant, he dove

David and Goliath

behind the nearest bush.

"You heard the giant!" King Saul yelled from behind the bush. "One of you cowards has to fight him. Line up, and choose who that will be."

"But . . ." said the few soldiers who were brave enough to speak.

"But nothing," King Saul shouted. "Go to it!"

David watched the Israelite soldiers line up on one side of the battlefield while the Philistine soldiers lined up on the other side. None of them went to Goliath who stood in the center.

"WHO'S IT GOING TO BE?" Goliath boomed, glaring at each of the Israelite soldiers, one by one.

"One of my soldiers had bet-ter speak up soon," King Saul hissed from his hiding place. He didn't notice the young shepherd boy who stood nearby.

"I'll fight Goliath," David whispered to King Saul.

King Saul peered out from behind the bush, noticing David for the first time. "What's that, boy?" he asked.

"I said 'I'll fight Goliath,'" David repeated confidently. He knew God would watch over him, and he didn't feel afraid at all.

"Run along home, boy," King Saul said. "This is no time for jokes. You're much too young and skinny and. . . ."

While the King babbled on and on, David picked up his staff, chose five smooth stones

David and Goliath

from a nearby stream, and put them into his bag. Then he walked boldly out to the battlefield. He didn't stop until he was face to face—actually, face to ankle—with Goliath.

"I'll fight you!" David shouted up at the giant. He had to yell it a few times before Goliath even heard him.

"IS THAT A MOUSE I HEAR?" Goliath asked, peering down at the ground. When he saw David, he began to laugh. "HA HA HA HA HA!" he roared. "DO YOU REALLY THINK YOU CAN KILL ME WITH THAT WIMPY SLINGSHOT?"

In the loudest voice he could muster, David said, "You come against me with a three-hundred-pound bronze sword and a five-hundred-pound iron spear. But I come against you in the name of God—the God of the people of Israel." Then quickly, he reached into his bag, pulled out a stone, and loaded his slingshot. David aimed and. . . .

SMACK! The stone hit Goliath right in the middle of his forehead. Goliath fell to the ground, face first, with a loud crash. David had won!

No one could believe their eyes— David's brothers, the other soldiers, and King Saul were completely stunned. When they got over their shock, they began to shout: "We're free! The Philistines are now are slaves! Young David won our battle!"

And so the Israelites celebrated. Little did they know then that the young, brave boy who slayed the giant would one day be their king.

The Lord is my shepherd; I shall not want.

He maketh me to lie down in green pastures:
he leadeth me beside the still waters.

He restoreth my soul: he leadeth me in
the paths of righteousness for his name's sake.

Yea, though I walk through the valley
of the shadow of death, I will fear no evil:
for thou art with me; thy rod and thy
staff they comfort me.

Thou preparest a table before me
in the presence of mine enemies:
thou anointest my head with oil:
my cup runneth over.

Surely goodness and mercy shall follow me all the days of my life: and I will dwell in the house of the Lord for ever.

PSALM 23

Protect me, O Lord,
My boat is so small,
And your sea is so big.

BRETON FISHERMEN'S PRAYER

Mask
Making

The wolf and the

lamb will feed

together, and the

lion will eat straw

like the ox.

ISAIAH 65:25

What did Daniel face in the lion's den? Where was the lost sheep hiding? Recreate favorite Bible stories by making masks! Read stories aloud while your children act out the parts.

Lion Mask

paper plate, scissors, glue, button or bottle cap, pipe cleaners, colored construction paper, yarn, popsicle stick

1. Cut out eye holes in the paper plate.
2. Glue on a button or bottle-cap nose and pipe cleaner whiskers.
3. Cut several strips of paper in various lengths. Glue the ends around the edge of the plate.
4. Cut several 6- to 8-inch pieces of yarn. Loop the ends together and glue layers around the mask face.
5. Make as many "mane" layers of paper and yarn as your mask will allow.
6. Glue a popsicle-stick handle to the bottom of the mask.
7. Hold it over child's face. Roar!!

Lamb Mask

paper plate, scissors, glue, button or bottle cap, pink felt, cotton balls, yarn

1. Cut out eye holes on the paper plate.
2. Glue on a button or bottle-cap nose.
3. Trim felt into floppy U-shaped ears and smaller U-shaped tongue. Glue in place.
4. Glue cotton-ball fleece all over the lamb's face.
5. Poke holes near the edge of plate where your ears would be. Tie on two pieces of yarn long enough for child's head.
6. Tie around head. Baa baa-a-aa!

A Walk in the Woods

Appreciate God's nature with your children by enjoying a walk through woods. Gather wildflowers and leaves to look at God's many designs.

Leaf Rubbings
leaves, lightweight paper, crayons

1. Arrange leaves on a flat surface, upside down. Make sure the undersides of the leaves (with the raised veins) are faceup.
2. Place a sheet of lightweight paper over the leaves.
3. Remove the paper wrapping from your crayons. Using the side of a crayon, rub the surface of the paper covering the leaves.
4. Experiment with different leaf collages and different colors.

Flower Pressing
Wildflowers, blank notebook, heavy books, glue, construction paper, clear adhesive plastic

1. Open a notebook and lay one plant flat on a left-handed page, exactly as you want it to dry. Turn about six pages and lay a second plant flat. Repeat until all your wildflowers are pressed.
2. Place the notebook in a safe, dry spot and stack a heavy pile of books on top of it.
3. Leave the notebook undisturbed for about two weeks.
4. Once your flowers are dry, use them to make note cards or bookmarks. Carefully glue them onto construction paper and let dry. For extra protection, cover them with clear adhesive plastic.

Then God said, "Let the land produce vegetation: seed-bearing plants and trees on the land that bear fruit with seed in it ...."

GENESIS 1:11

Daniel and the Lions

any years ago, a Persian king chose the three smartest men of his kingdom to be his advisors. One of these advisors was a young man named Daniel. Unlike the king and the other two advisors, Daniel was a Jew. All his life he prayed to God and followed his laws, and he was grateful that God had blessed him with wisdom.

It didn't take long for the king to realize that Daniel was wiser and more dependable than the other two advisors. One day he called Daniel to his throne.

"Daniel," he said, "from now on, you are in charge of my kingdom."

"But what about your other two advisors?" Daniel asked.

"I don't trust them as I trust you," said the king.

When the king's other advisors heard about Daniel's new position, they were very jealous. So they plotted against him.

"We must discover something Daniel has done wrong," said an advisor. "Then we can spread word of it throughout the kingdom. When the king hears of it, he'll get rid of Daniel once and for all."

"But he never does anything wrong," the other advisor said. "He doesn't steal, he doesn't cheat, he doesn't lie...all he does is pray to his God three times a day."

The two advisors thought and thought until they were completely exhausted. They came up with a plan.

Daniel and the Lions

"Your Majesty," one advisor said, "you are very much like a god, and we think you should be worshiped like one."

The king thought about this for a moment and shrugged. "If you say so," he said, "after all, you are my advisors."

"Yes, we are," said the other advisor, "which is why we think you should sign this order." He handed the king an order, and the king read it aloud.

"FOR THE NEXT THIRTY DAYS, ALL MEN MUST PRAY ONLY TO THE KING. IF A MAN IS CAUGHT PRAYING TO ANOTHER GOD, HE WILL BE THROWN INTO THE LIONS' DEN TO DIE." When the king finished reading, he shrugged.

"Sounds good to me," he said, and signed his royal signature.

By the next day, everyone in the kingdom, including Daniel, had read the order. But instead of obeying it like everyone else, Daniel continued praying to God as he always had. Three times a day—morning, noon, and night—he knelt by his window and thanked God for all he'd been blessed with. He prayed that his people could live in Jerusalem, that they would have enough to eat and drink, and that they would be blessed with good health.

A few days after the royal order

came out, the two advisors decided to spy on Daniel. At noon, they climbed a tree outside his window and, hidden by the leaves, peered inside. They saw exactly what they had hoped to see—Daniel still praying to his one and only God. Excited by what they witnessed, the two advisors raced back to the king.

"Remember that order you signed?" they asked breathlessly. "You know—the one that forbids people to worship any god but yourself?" The king nodded.

"Well," they said, grinning slyly. "Guess who didn't obey that law."

"I'm too busy to play guessing games," the king said sternly, "but whoever it was must be thrown into the lions' den."

"It was Daniel!" the advisors announced. "He still prays to his God."

The king was very sorry to hear this, for he was very fond of Daniel and didn't mind that he prayed to his own God. "I've been tricked!" he yelled at the grinning advisors. But he knew there was nothing he could do. A royal order was a royal order.

The following afternoon, two robust guards brought Daniel to the king.

"I'm terribly sorry, Daniel," said the king. "If I had known this would happen I never would have signed such an order."

"I understand," Daniel said calmly. "But I'm not afraid. My God will watch over me."

"I hope your God can save you,"

the king said doubtfully. Then he bowed his head, for he couldn't bear to watch the guards lead Daniel away.

GRRRR! roared the lions when Daniel and the guards arrived. The lions licked their black lips and drooled onto the den floor.

"One...two...three," the guards counted, and pushed Daniel in. Then they quickly rolled a heavy boulder across the entrance so Daniel could not escape.

That night, the king's advisors were so excited they couldn't sleep. The king couldn't sleep either—but for a different reason. He tossed and turned and worried about Daniel. By now, he thought, Daniel has probably been torn to shreds by the lions.

At dawn, the king hurried to the lions' den. He put his ear to the heavy boulder that blocked the entrance and listened. He heard nothing but silence. Could the lions be sleeping after their tasty meal, he wondered, shivering with horror.

"Daniel!" he called. "Oh, Daniel. Has your God rescued you?" Not expecting an answer he began to sob.

"Yes, Your Majesty!" Daniel called from inside. "God knew I was inno-cent so he protected me. He sent an angel to shut the mouths of the lions. That's why they're so quiet this morning!"

The king couldn't believe his ears! His tears of sorrow turned into tears of joy, and he called for the guards to come at once. "Remove this boulder!" he ordered. "Daniel is alive!"

The guards followed the king's orders, and minutes later Daniel climbed out of the cave. "Good morning, Your Majesty," he said calmly. There wasn't a wound or a bite or even a tiny scratch on him.

The king ordered the guards to fetch the two advisors. When they arrived and saw Daniel healthy and whole, they began to shiver with terror. But that didn't stop the king from ordering that now they be

thrown into the lions' den.

GRRRRRR! GRRRRR! the lions roared, now that there were no more angels to hold their mouths shut. They gobbled up both advisors in only two seconds flat!

The king was so overjoyed about Daniel being safe that he sent out a royal order to everyone in the kingdom. FROM NOW ON, it said, YOU ARE TO RESPECT THE GOD OF DANIEL. FOR HE IS THE ONLY GOD THERE IS. HE SAVED DANIEL FROM THE LIONS.

For many years after that, Daniel continued to be in charge of the kingdom and was the king's one and only advisor. And three times a day, Daniel prayed to his one and only God. ✳

Prayers

Day by day, dear Lord, of Thee
Three things I pray:
To see Thee more clearly,
To love Thee more dearly,
To follow Thee more nearly,
Day by day.

St. Richard of Chichester

The Wind and the Sun

The wind and the sun once had spirited words as to which had the most strength. "I give the world light and heat," beamed the sun. "Without my rays, the land would have no plants, and frost would cover all the earth."

"I put forth gusts in the sails of ships," howled the wind. "I blow rain clouds to and fro and can cause a terrible, terrible storm."

Just then, by chance a man walked by. The sun and wind agreed to a challenge: He who got this man's cloak off first should win the day. The wind was the first to try. He blew with all his might and made a fierce blast, but the man wrapped his cloak all the more tightly around himself. Next came the sun, who burst out with his warm beams and cast his bright rays on the man. Before long, the man grew very warm with the heat. He gladly parted with his cloak and flung it to the ground.

Kind means are best.

Let There Be Light

Start the week by celebrating the first day of creation. Make a mobile frame out of a tree branch with many twigs and string on heavenly bodies you make. Imagine with your children that the finished mobile is the hand of God, holding the sun, moon, and stars.

God saw that the

light was good, and

he separated the light

from the darkness.

GENESIS 1:4

Shining Sun

red, orange & yellow tissue paper, scissors, glue, clear plastic round lid, hole punch, string

1. Draw triangular sunrays half the length of the lid on tissue paper. Cut out.
2. Spread a thin layer of glue on the lid. Paste on tissue rays to create a circle of colored rays.
4. Shine light through lid to see different colors.
5. Punch a hole near edge. Tie string through hole and tie to branch.

Foil Moon

cardboard, marker, scissors, aluminum foil, hole punch, string

1. Draw crescent and full moons on cardboard. Cut out.
2. Wrap each completely with aluminum foil.
3. Punch a hole near edge. Tie string through hole and tie to branch.

Glittering Stars

cardboard, marker, scissors, glue, glitter (gold, silver, blue), hole punch, string

1. Draw different-sized stars on cardboard. Vary them by making longer or shorter points.
2. Spread a thin layer of glue on top.
3. Sprinkle each with a different color glitter. Let dry. Repeat on other side.
4. Punch a hole near edge. Tie string through hole and tie to branch.

Shining Light

Let your light shine! Help your children make personalized candleholders. Light a candle during evening prayers. At Christmastime, go caroling with windproof tin lanterns.

Stained Glass Lantern

glue, glass pint jars, colored tissue paper, scissors, paintbrush, candle

1. Squeeze 2 tablespoons of glue into a jar. Thin with water until the consistency is like milk.
2. Cut different shapes, sizes, and colors of tissue paper.
3. Brush the outside of a second jar with glue solution.
4. Overlap the tissue paper shapes on the glass and brush over them with glue solution. Let dry.
5. Place a candle in the bottom of the glass. Light and watch the room fill with color.

Tin Can Lantern

large tin can, marker, large nail, hammer, wire coat hanger, candle

1. Fill the can with water and place in a freezer until frozen.
2. With a marker, draw stars, moon, or sun patterns on the outside of the can.
3. Carefully poke holes along your markings with a hammer and nail.
4. For the handle, poke two holes near the top of the can directly opposite one another.
5. Melt and remove the ice.
6. Bend the hanger and loop the ends through the handle holes. Twist ends to secure.
7. Place a candle in your lantern.

Let your light shine before men, that they may see your good deeds and praise your Father in heaven.

MATTHEW 5:16

233

This Little Light of Mine

This lit-tle light of mine, I'm gon-na let it shine.

This lit-tle light of mine, I'm gon-na let it shine, let it

shine, let it shine, let it shine.

2. Hide it under a bushel? NO!
   I'm gonna let it shine.
   Hide it under a bushel? NO!
   I'm gonna let it shine, let it shine,
   let it shine, let it shine.

3. Don't let Satan blow it out,
   I'm gonna let it shine,
   Don't let Satan blow it out,
   I'm gonna let it shine, let it shine,
   let it shine, let it shine.

234

Heavenly Sunshine

Heav - en - ly sun - shine, heav - en - ly
sun - shine, Flood - ing my soul with glo - ry di - -
vine, _____ Heav - en - ly sun - shine, heav - en - ly
sun - shine, Hal - le - lu - jah, Je - sus is mine.

Where Is Heaven?

by Bliss Carman

Where is Heaven? Is it not
Just a friendly garden plot,
Walled with stone and roofed with sun,
Where the days pass one by one
Not too fast and not too slow,
Looking backward as they go
At the beauties left behind
To transport the pensive mind.

Does not Heaven begin that day
When the eager heart can say,
Surely God is in this place,
I have seen Him face to face
In the loveliness of flowers,
In the service of the showers,
And His voice has talked to me
In the sunlit apple tree.

Verses on Heaven

The Lord is in his holy temple; the Lord is on his heavenly throne. He observes the sons of men; his eyes examine them.

PSALM 11:4

But store up for yourselves treasures in heaven, where moth and rust do not destroy, and where thieves do not break in and steal.

MATTHEW 6:20

In my Father's house are many rooms; if it were not so, I would have told you. I am going there to prepare a place for you.

JOHN 14:2

I tell you the truth, unless you change and become like little children, you will never enter the kingdom of heaven.

MATTHEW 18:3

The Pearl of Great Price

One day, a merchant entered an old, dusty gem shop. He had been there many times before, for it was where he bought many of the gems he sold in his own shop. Over the years, he had bought thousands of small gems—rubies, emeralds, sapphires, opals, pearls, and other shiny stones. Some of the gems had been far from perfect, others had been near perfect, but every single one of them had at least one scratch, nick, spot, or other flaw.

The merchant spent many hours sorting through dusty boxes. At the end of the day, he left the shop tired and discouraged. He had not found what he was looking for. As soon as he stepped outside, he saw an old man sitting on the road with a box in his hands. There, in the box, was the most beautiful, magnificent pearl—without a single flaw! It was perfect. It was the gem he had been looking for all his life.

He begged the old man to wait. Quickly, he rushed home and sold everything he owned—his shop, his home, and even his camel. Then, he returned to the old man with the money and bought the perfect pearl, for he treasured it more than anything else in the world.

So too should you search for and treasure the kingdom of God.

> *The kingdom of heaven is like a merchant looking for fine pearls.*
>
> MATTHEW 13:45

241

Jonah and the Fish

any years ago, there lived a man named Jonah. Jonah was one of God's people, and one day God spoke to him.

"Jonah," God said. "I want you to go to the city of Ninevah. Tell the people that I have seen their wicked ways. Say that if they don't change I will punish them."

Now Jonah had heard plenty of stories about the people of Ninevah— and none of them were good. They were the Israelites' worst enemies. If Jonah went there, they might beat him up or throw him into prison for no good reason. So, instead of obeying God, Jonah ran away.

Jonah hitched a ride to the port of Joppa, where a large ship was about to set sail. As the ship's crew loaded on the last of the cargo, Jonah climbed aboard, paid his fare, and made his way into the lower cabin. When he found a tiny room with a cot, he took off his sandals and lay down. By the time the ship left the port, he was fast asleep.

Meanwhile, on the upper deck, the sailors were using all their strength to pull in the sails. As soon as they lost all sight of land, God sent down a strong gust of wind. But that was only the beginning! While Jonah snoozed down below, the wind became so fierce it made giant waves that caused the ship to rock violently. While Jonah snored, lightning flashed, and—CR-A-ACK BOOM— thunder roared. Then huge raindrops began to fall from the darkening sky.

Jonah and the Fish

"The ship's going to split in two!" cried the captain, slipping and sliding across the deck.

"We're all going to drown!" cried a sailor, shielding his eyes from the streaming rain.

CR-A-ACK BOOM! CR-A-ACK CR-A-ACK BOOM! went the thunder.

Terrified, the sailors began praying to their own gods. That's when the captain remembered seeing a stranger come aboard. He went down below and found Jonah sleeping soundly.

"Wake up!" the captain yelled as he shook Jonah awake. "Get up and pray to your God like everyone else. Maybe he can save us from this violent storm." Then the captain hurried back to the deck to be with his crew.

"Violent storm?" Jonah said, rubbing his eyes. Just then the cot slid from one side of the room to the other. He saw a burst of lightning through a porthole. CR-A-ACK CR-A-ACK BOOM! Thunder shook the ship.

"Oh, no!" Jonah gasped, suddenly remembering where he was and what he had done. He realized that God must have sent the storm to punish him. He raced to the upper deck and found the sailors huddled together, trying to figure out which of them

243

Jonah and the Fish

was responsible for their horrible luck.

"Maybe it's his fault!" yelled a sailor, pointing directly at Jonah.

"Who are you?" asked another sailor. "Where did you come from? Who is your God?"

"I am a Jew," Jonah said. "I worship the God who made this world we live in. But at the moment, I am running away from him."

The sailors stared at Jonah with horror. They had heard about Jews and their mighty, powerful God. They shivered with terror.

The captain, too, was terrified, but he was also very angry. "Why should my crew and I have to suffer for your mistakes?" he shouted at Jonah. "Now your God will kill us all—unless you know of something we can do to save ourselves."

As the sea became rougher and rougher, Jonah was silent. He felt terrible that so many people were suffering just because he had run away from God.

"You're right," he finally said to the captain. "This violent storm is all my fault. If I hadn't boarded your ship, you wouldn't be in this situation. Have your sailors throw me into the sea and maybe my God will leave you alone."

But the sailors would do no such

thing. If they threw Jonah—one of God's people—overboard, they were sure his God would punish them. Instead, they each grabbed an oar and tried to row back to land.

Still they had no luck. As they rowed, the sea became even wilder, and most of the oars drifted out to sea.

"Please, God!" the sailors prayed—this time to Jonah's God. "Don't punish us for taking the life of one of your people. We have no choice!" Next they picked up Jonah and counted—one, two, three—and tossed him into the sea.

Instantly, the sea became calm. The waves stopped raging, and the ship stopped rocking. The rain stopped pouring, and hints of a sunrise lit up the horizon. The captain

and the sailors thanked God and returned to their duties. But Jonah sank down, down, down. . . .

The water was cold and dark, and Jonah could barely hold his breath. His foot got caught in a clump of seaweed. Then just as he untangled himself, everything darkened in shadow. Jonah looked up and found himself face to face with a huge, dark fish. Before he could swim away, the fish opened up his mouth wide and . . . GULP!

The fish swallowed the clump of seaweed, a school of fish, and Jonah!

"It's dark in here!" Jonah cried, now able to breathe. (God must have made this possible.) Jonah was even more afraid now than he'd been in the storm. His eyes slowly grew used to the darkness as he floated around the big, hollow belly of the fish. He stared with awe at the colorful fish, horseshoe crabs, pieces of coral, clams, oysters, seashells, pebbles, and the other sea life the fish had swallowed. It was quite a strange experience!

As Jonah sloshed this way and that inside the fish's belly, he prayed desperately. "Please help me, God," he begged. "I'm sorry for disobeying you. If you rescue me, I'll do anything you say." He prayed and prayed for three days and three nights until finally, God commanded the fish to open his mouth and spit Jonah onto dry land.

And the fish obeyed him!

In a forceful rush of water, Jonah flew out of the fish's mouth and landed along with several other pieces of sea life on a sandy beach. As he squinted in the bright sunlight and tried to get his balance, God spoke to him.

"I want you to go to the city of Ninevah," he said. "Tell the people that I have seen their wicked ways, and warn them that if they don't change, I will punish them."

This time Jonah obeyed.

Here I Am, Lord

Words by Daniel Schutte

Verse:

I, the Lord of sea and sky, I have heard my peo-ple cry.

All who dwell in dark and sin my hand will save.

I who made the stars of night, I will make their dark - ness bright.

Refrain:

Who will bear my light to them? Whom shall I send? ___ Here I

am, Lord. ____ Is it I, lord? ____ I have
heard you call - ing in the night. ____ I will
go, Lord, ____ if you lead me. ____ I will
hold your peo - ple in my heart. ____

2. I, the Lord of snow and rain,
I have borne my people's pain.
I have wept for love of them.
They turn a-way.
I will break their hearts of stone,
give them hearts for love a-lone.
I will speak my word to them.
Whom shall I send?
Refrain

3. I, the Lord of wind and flame,
I will tend the poor and lame.
I will set a feast for them.
My hand will save.
Finest bread I will pro-vide
till their hearts be sat-is-fied.
I will give my life to them.
Whom shall I send?
Refrain

God Make My Life
a Little Light

by M. Bentham-Edwardsthat

God make my life a little light,
    Within the world to glow;
A tiny flame that burneth bright
    Wherever I may go.

God make my life a little flower,
    That giveth joy to all,
Content to bloom in native bower,
    Although its place be small.

God make my life a little staff,
    Whereon the weak may rest,
That so what health and strength I have
    May serve my neighbors best.

The Prodigal Son

Once there was a hardworking farmer and his two sons. When his youngest son was grown up, he went to his father and asked, "Dear father, I wish to start a life for myself. Please, give me my share of the family's money now." Although it pained him, the father agreed. The young man, ecstatic from his fortune, embarked on adventures he couldn't afford. It wasn't long before he was poor and hungry.

The young man longed to return home, even if he had to work his father's fields as a servant. When he returned, he was embraced by his father who was crying from joy. The father called to the servants to dress his son with his finest robes and to feast on fattened calf in celebration.

When the older son learned that his little brother came back, after having spent all the money, only to be happily welcomed back by his father, the older son became enraged. "Father, how could you do this? Since when have I tasted fattened calf under your roof, in all the years that I have faithfully worked with you?" The man smiled, "My son, I never had any fears for you. You have always been by my side, and all that is mine is yours. Come, your brother has returned. What was lost has now been found. Let us rejoice."

> *For this son of mine was dead and is alive again; he was lost and is found.*
>
> LUKE 15:24

Prayers

First the seed and then the grain;
Thank you, God, for sun and rain.
First the flour and then the bread;
Thank you, God, that we are fed.
Thank you, God, for all your care;
help us all to share and share.

Amen.

Jesus is Born

any years ago, in the town of Nazareth, a man named Joseph—a descendant of King David—and a woman named Mary planned to get married. A few weeks before the wedding was to take place, the Emperor Caesar Augustus sent out an important notice saying that a census would be taken. (A census is when all the people of a place are counted to find out how many there are.) "In order to do this," the order read, "all men must return to their place of birth." So Joseph and Mary packed their belongings and set off for Bethlehem, the place where Joseph had been born. It was a long ride, and Mary was very uncomfortable. You see, her belly was very, very big because she

was going to have a baby—not Joseph's baby, but God's baby. Knowing his soon-to-be wife had a holy baby inside of her, Joseph took extra good care of her.

When they arrived in Bethlehem, the streets were noisier, dustier, and more crowded than Joseph remembered them to be. Men and women flooded the marketplace, vendors shouted out their wares, boys and girls played catch with stray pieces of fruit, dogs barked, cats meowed, and mice scurried under everybody's feet. Joseph was about to tell Mary that he recognized very few people when. . . .

"Joseph!" Mary moaned. "I just felt a pain in my belly. The baby is about to be born!" She winced and

waited for another pain to pass.

Quickly, Joseph led their donkey away from the crowds toward the outskirts of town. "We must find a place for you to be comfortable," he said, feeling nervous and excited at the same time. As they rode along, Mary clutched her belly, wincing with pain every few minutes. Soon they reached an old inn.

"Do you have any rooms?" he asked the innkeeper while Mary waited outside. "My wife is about to have a baby."

"Sorry," said the innkeeper, "but every room is full. Lots of people have come to Bethlehem because of the census."

Joseph returned to Mary, whose pains were coming every few seconds now, and they rode to another inn— but it too was full. So were the next three inns they tried. The last innkeeper took one look at Mary and suggested they go to the stables behind the inn. "At least it's quiet back there," he said kindly.

Just as they reached the stables, Mary let out a wail and minutes later gave birth to a tiny baby boy. "His name is Jesus," she said to Joseph. And they both wept with joy as they dressed God's Son in old cloths and placed him in a manger. (A manger is a trough filled with hay for animals to eat from.)

That evening, out in a pasture near Bethlehem, three shepherds watched their flocks. As the sky darkened around their cattle and sheep, they suddenly saw a shimmery light, which got brighter and brighter until the entire pasture was lit up!

"That's the brightest star I've ever seen!" cried one of the shepherds, shielding his eyes.

"It's bigger than a star!" said another shepherd. "And it's getting bigger and brighter every second."

"Shhhh," said the third shepherd. "Do you hear that lovely music?"

The other shepherds nodded as they listened to a sweet melody that seemed to come from the brightness.

Suddenly, a beautiful angel appeared before them and they gasped with terror!

"Do not be afraid," the angel said in a soft, velvety voice. "I've come with joyful news. Today, in the town of Bethlehem, the Son of God has been born. He will be the King of the Jews. You must go and see for yourselves."

"W-where will we find him?" asked one of the shepherds. (The others were too filled with awe to speak, for they knew this angel had been sent by God.)

"Go to the inn at the farthest end of town," said the angel. "Behind it is a stable. You'll find the Baby Jesus in a manger." Then the angel disappeared and the sky was dark.

"Let's go to Bethlehem!" the three shepherds said at the same time. They gathered their flocks and headed into town under a starlit sky. A few hours later they reached the stable. Mary was busy feeding God's Son while Joseph watched with love in his eyes.

As the shepherds watched this beautiful scene, a warm, peaceful feeling came over them.

It was true! The shepherds now knew. The King of the Jews had been born! They spread the joyful news all over town, and crowds of people came to see God's Son for themselves. As they gazed at the tiny baby in the manger, their eyes filled with tears. They were very grateful that

God had blessed them with such a wonderful gift.

Meanwhile, on the same night Baby Jesus was born, three wise men in the east were looking up at the stars. These wise men had spent years studying astronomy, and they were very familiar with the night sky.

"I've never seen that one before," one of the wise men said with surprise as he pointed to an especially bright star.

"That star is a sign from God," another wise man said with excitement.

"God's letting us know that his Son, the King of the Jews, has been born!" said the third wise man.

With that, the three wise men packed up their few belongings, including special gifts for the baby, and climbed on their camels. Then they set off for Jerusalem. You see, at that time Jerusalem was the most beautiful and popular city and they assumed they would find Baby Jesus there. As they rode through the hot, dry desert, the wise men grew more and more excited. They couldn't wait to worship their new King!

The three wise men traveled for many weeks. When they finally arrived in Jerusalem, they made an appointment with King Herod, Jerusalem's mean and jealous ruler, for they thought he would know where they could find God's tiny Son.

"Your Majesty," said one of the wise men. "Where is the baby who has been born King of the Jews?"

King Herod looked confused, for he hadn't heard about Baby Jesus.

"We saw his star in the east and have come to worship him," another wise man explained.

"Worship him?" King Herod shouted angrily. "I'm the only king who should be worshiped!" Then he sent the wise men out and called together all his advisors and priests and teachers of the law. "Has anyone heard of

261

a baby boy that has been born to be King of the Jews?" he asked nervously.

"I have!" said one of his advisors. "The child lives with his parents in Bethlehem."

King Herod frowned. He ordered a servant to fetch the three wise men. "The baby boy you're searching for is in Bethlehem," he said when they once again stood before his throne. "Go there and find out the exact place he lives. Then come back and tell me all about him."

"But why do you want to know about him?" one of the wise men asked.

"So that I too may go and worship him," said King Herod. This, of course, was a lie. He really just wanted to learn more about this extraor-dinary infant.

That evening, the three wise men climbed on their camels and headed toward Bethlehem. This time they knew exactly where they were going, for now they followed the bright star that had been in the sky on the night Baby Jesus was born. Brighter than anything else in the night sky, the star led them right to the quaint cottage where Joseph, Mary, and Baby Jesus were now living.

The wise men tied their camels to the outside gate, went to the front door, and knocked. Seconds later,

Mary invited them inside.

"We've come a long way," said one of the wise men, as he wiped his boots on the doormat.

"A bright star led us here," said another wise man, listening for the sounds of a baby.

"We'd like to worship our new King," said the third wise man.

"Follow me," Mary said, and she led them into a room where Joseph sat in front of a glowing fire. When they saw Baby Jesus, cooing and smiling in the cradle beside Joseph, the wise men sunk to their knees, overcome by a feeling of pure love and joy.

After several minutes of silence, the wise men, one by one, presented Baby Jesus with treasures.

"This is for you, great King," said one wise man, placing a bag of gold at the foot of the cradle. Then he moved away and the next wise man took his place.

"You will be the greatest of all men," the second wise man said to Baby Jesus. He placed a jar of myrrh next to the gold. (Myrrh is a special perfume that can only be worn by important men.) Then he moved away to make room for the last wise man.

"This incense will make the air sweet," the third wise man explained to Mary and Joseph, placing a small jar between the gold and the myrrh. "Incense is pleasing to God. The tiny king in this cradle is both man and God."

Mary and Joseph thanked the wise men warmly. Then they all bowed their heads and prayed to God. They thanked him for bringing Baby Jesus—King of the Jews—into the world. Then the wise men left, feeling wonderfully blessed.

That night, the wise men slept at an inn where they all had the same strange dream. In the dream, a voice warned them not to return to King Herod. When the wise men woke up, they knew that the voice in the

dream belonged to God. He had sent them a warning. So instead of traveling back to Jerusalem as they had planned, the three wise men went home along a different route.

King Herod eventually heard all about God's very special son—he was all anyone in the kingdom ever talked about. The story of Baby Jesus' birth was told over and over and over again. No one, including the three wise men, the three shepherds, Mary, or Joseph, would ever forget what happened on that miraculous night. Even today, all over the world, the birthday of Baby Jesus is still celebrated. But now it's known as Christmas.

Angels We Have Heard on High

An - gels we have heard on high, sweet - ly sing - ing o'er the plain,

And the moun - tains in re - ply, Ech - o - ing their joy - ous strain.

Glo - - - - - - - - - - - - - - - - ri - a in ex - cel - sis

De - o, Glo - ri - a

in ex - cel - sis De - - - - o! _____

2. Shepherds, why this jubilee?
   Why your joyful strains prolong?
   What the gladsome tidings be
   Which inspire your heav'nly song?

Refrain

3. Come to Bethlehem and see
   Him whose birth the angels sing;
   Come adore on bended knee
   Christ, the Lord, the new-born King.

Refrain

4. See Him in a manger laid,
   Whom the choir of angels praise;
   Holy Spirit, lend thine aid,
   While our hearts in love we raise.

Refrain

The Lamb

by William Blake

Little lamb, who made thee?
Dost thou know who made thee,
Gave thee life, and made thee feed
By the stream and o'er the mead?
Gave thee clothing of delight,
Softest clothing, wooly, bright?
Gave thee such a tender voice,
Making all the vales rejoice?
Little lamb, who made thee?
Doest thou know who made thee,

Little lamb, I'll tell thee;
Little lamb, I'll tell thee:
He is called by thy name,
For He calls Himself a lamb.
He is meek, and He is mild;
He became a little child:
I a child, and thou a lamb,
We are called by His name.
Little lamb, God bless thee!
Little lamb, God bless thee!

The Ten Maidens

There were once ten young women who were invited to the wedding of their dear friend. They were all eager to meet the groom who was to sweep the bride off her feet. When the day of the procession came, the ten women made preparations, but only five of them were wise enough to bring extra jars of oil for their lamps. The other five only took the oil already in their lamps.

They were all excited to see the ceremony, but the procession was a long time coming. When night came, the waiting young women had all fallen asleep. Around midnight, they heard a shout, "Ho! Here comes the bridegroom!" The women rose and excitedly opened their lamps, but only the five wise ones still had oil left to burn. The other five foolish women had lamps that were burned out. Even though they felt sorry, the wise women could not spare any oil because then there wouldn't be enough for any of them.

The poor, foolish women had no choice but to go back and buy more oil. By the time they arrived with their lit lamps, the guests had already all arrived and the doors were shut. They knocked and knocked, but they could not get in. The ceremony had already begun.

Be prepared for the kingdom of heaven.

> *Keep watch, because you do not know the day or the hour.*
>
> MATTHEW 25:13

The Selfish Giant

by Oscar Wilde

very afternoon, as they were coming from school, the children used to go and play in the Giant's garden. It was a large lovely garden, with soft green grass. Here and there over the grass stood beautiful flowers like stars, and there were twelve peach trees that in the springtime broke out into delicate blossoms of pink and pearl, and in the autumn bore rich fruit. The birds sat on the trees and sang so sweetly that the children used to stop their games in order to listen to them. "How happy we are here!" they cried to each other.

One day the Giant came back. He had been to visit his friend the Cornish ogre, and had stayed with him for seven years. After the seven years were over he had said all that he had to say, for his conversation was limited, and he determined to return to his own castle. When he arrived he saw the children playing in the garden.

What are you doing here?" he cried in a very gruff voice, and the children ran away.

"My own garden is my own garden," said the Giant; "anyone can

The Selfish Giant

understand that, and I will allow nobody to play in it but myself." So he
built a high wall all round it, and put up a notice-board.

TRESPASSERS WILL BE PROSECUTED

He was a very selfish Giant.

The poor children had now nowhere to play. They tried to play on
the road, but the road was very dusty and full of hard
stones, and they did not like it. They used to wander
round the high wall when their lessons were over, and
talk about the beautiful garden inside. "How happy
we were there," they said to each other.

Then the Spring came, and all over the coun-
try there were little blossoms and little birds.
Only in the garden of the Selfish Giant it was
still winter. The birds did not care to sing in it as
there were no children, and the trees forgot to blossom.
Once a beautiful flower put its head out from the grass, but when it
saw the notice-board it was so sorry for the children that it slipped
back into the ground again, and went off to sleep. The only people who

The Selfish Giant

were pleased were the Snow and the Frost. "Spring has forgotten this garden," they cried, "so we will live here all the year round." The Snow covered up the grass with her great white cloak, and the Frost painted all the trees silver. . . .

"I cannot understand why the Spring is so late in coming," said the Selfish Giant, as he sat at the window and looked out at his cold white garden; "I hope there will be a change in the weather."

But the Spring never came, nor the Summer. The Autumn gave golden fruit to every garden, but to the Giant's garden she gave none. "He is too selfish," she said. So it was always Winter there, and the North Wind, and the Hail, and the Frost, and the Snow danced about through the trees.

One morning the Giant was lying awake in bed when he heard some lovely music. It sounded so sweet to his ears that he thought it must be the King's musicians passing by. It was really only a little linnet singing outside his window, but it was so long since he had heard a bird sing in his garden that it seemed to him to be the most beautiful music in the world. Then the Hail stopped dancing over his head, and the North Wind ceased roaring, and a delicious perfume came to him through the open casement. "I believe the Spring has come at last," said the Giant; and he jumped out of bed and looked out.

What did he see?

He saw a most wonderful sight. Through a little hole in the wall the children had crept in, and they were sitting in the branches of the trees. In every tree that he could see there was a little child. And the trees were so glad to have the children back again that they had covered themselves with blossoms, and were waving their arms gently above the children's heads. The birds were flying about and twittering with delight, and the flowers were looking up through the green grass and laughing. It was a lovely scene, only in one corner it was still winter. It was the farthest corner of the garden, and in it was standing a little boy. He was so small that he could not reach up to the branches of the tree, and he was wandering all round it, crying bitterly. The poor tree was still quite covered with frost and snow, and the North Wind was blowing and roaring above it. "Climb up! little boy," said the Tree, and it bent its branches down as low as it could; but the boy was too tiny.

And the Giant's heart melted as he looked out. "How selfish I have

The Selfish Giant

been!" he said; "now I know why the Spring would not come here. I will put that poor little boy on the top of the tree, and then I will knock down the wall, and my garden shall be the children's playground for ever and ever." He was really very sorry for what he had done.

So he crept downstairs and opened the front door quite softly, and went out into the garden. But when the children saw him they were so frightened that they all ran away, and the garden became winter again. Only the little boy did not run, for his eyes were so full of tears that he did not see the Giant coming. And the Giant stole up behind him and took him gently in his hand, and put him up into the tree. And the tree broke at once into blossom, and the birds came and sang on it, and the little boy stretched out his two arms and flung them round the Giant's neck, and kissed him. And the other children, when they saw that the Giant was not wicked any longer, came running back, and with them came the Spring. "It is your garden now, little children," said the Giant, and he took a great axe and knocked down the wall. And when the people were going to market at twelve o'clock they found the Giant playing with the children in the most beautiful garden they had ever seen.

All day long they played, and in the evening they came to the Giant to bid him good-bye.

The Selfish Giant

"But where is your little companion?" he said: "the boy I put into the tree." The Giant loved him the best because he had kissed him.

"We don't know," answered the children; "he has gone away."

"You must tell him to be sure and come here tomorrow," said the Giant. But the children said that they did not know where he lived, and had never seen him before; and the Giant felt very sad.

Every afternoon, when school was over, the children came and played with the Giant. But the little boy whom the Giant loved was never seen again. The Giant was very kind to all the children, yet he longed for his first little friend, and often spoke of him. "How I would like to see him!" he used to say.

Years went over, and the Giant grew very old and feeble. He could not play about any more, so he sat in a huge armchair, and watched the children at their games, and admired his garden. "I have many beautiful flowers," he said; "but the children are the most beautiful flowers of all."

One winter morning he looked out of his window as he was dressing. He did not hate the Winter now, for he knew that it was merely the Spring asleep, and that the flowers were resting.

Suddenly he rubbed his eyes in wonder, and looked and looked. It certainly was a marvelous sight. In the farthest corner of the garden was a tree quite covered with lovely white blossoms. Its branches were all golden, and silver fruit hung down from them, and underneath it stood the little boy he had loved.

Downstairs ran the Giant in great joy, and out into the garden. He hastened across the grass, and came near to the child. And when he came quite close his face grew red with anger, and he said, "Who hath dared to wound thee?" For on the palms of the child's hands were the prints of two nails, and the prints of two nails were on the little feet.

"Who hath dared to wound thee?" cried the Giant; "tell me, that I may take my big sword and slay him."

"Nay!" answered the child; "but these are the wounds of Love."

"Who art thou?" said the Giant, and a strange awe fell on him, and he knelt before the little child.

And the child smiled on the Giant, and said to him, "You let me play once in your garden, today you shall come with me to my garden, which is Paradise."

And when the children ran in that afternoon, they found the Giant lying dead under the tree, all covered with white blossoms.

Go Tell It on the Mountain

Go tell it on the moun-tain, O-ver the hills and ev-'ry-where; ___ Go tell it on the moun-tain, that Je-sus Christ is born! When I was a seek-er, I sought both night and day. I

asked the Lord to help me, And

he showed me the way.

Go tell it on the moun - tain,

O - ver the hills and ev - - - 'ry - where;

Go tell it on the moun - tain, that

Je - sus Christ is born!

Nativity

They saw the child

with his mother

Mary, and they

bowed down and

worshiped him.

MATTHEW 2:11

This Christmas, make a nativity scene. Turn an open shoebox onto its side and fill the bottom with straw for an instant stable. Make barnyard sheep out of salt dough (see page 56) and cotton. Then add the cast of characters here.

Three Wise Men

cardboard, scissors, glue, beads, pinecones, acorns, pipe cleaners, yarn, dried corn, dried herbs or flowers

1. Cut a cardboard circle about the same circumference as the pinecones for the base.
2. Glue two beads onto the circle for feet. Let dry.
3. Glue the pinecone body to the feet. Let dry.
4. Glue on an acorn head and pipe cleaner arms.
5. Add yarn for hair and beards. Glue corn, herbs, and flowers onto the hands for gifts.

Baby Jesus

felt, salt dough (see page 56), seeds, walnut shell half

1. Cut a triangular scrap of felt for a baby blanket.
2. Roll a small ball of dough for the baby's head. Press in two seeds for eyes.
4. Lay the head on one corner of the fabric. Fold the other two corners over each other.
5. Tuck the baby in the walnut-shell manger.

Mary and Joseph

different-sized stones, poster paint, yarn, glue, cloth

1. Glue three small stones of increasing size on top of each other. Repeat. (For a sitting Mary, use a flat stone on the bottom of one figure.) Let dry.
2. Paint on faces and glue on yarn for hair.
3. Tie triangular pieces of cloth for a kerchief for Mary's head and cloaks for both figures.

Jesus at the Temple

or years, Joseph and Mary went to Jerusalem for the Passover Feast. When Jesus was twelve years old, they decided he was old enough to go, too.

Jesus was very excited about the journey—he had never been to a city as big as Jerusalem before! When the day came, he woke up early and helped his parents prepare for the trip. He fed the donkey, loaded bundles onto its back, and helped his mother, Mary, climb aboard. Finally, they set off to meet the others—for Jesus and his family weren't the only travelers. Almost the entire town of Nazareth was going along with them!

Jesus' family joined a line of travelers—some on camels, some on donkeys, some on horses—and they set off for the city of Jerusalem. The seventy-mile journey took a little over two days. The men and women spent most of the time riding, while the children ran, hopped, and skipped alongside the group.

As they neared Jerusalem, sweet aromas from kitchens all over town floated out to greet them. It made Jesus remember what he'd been told about Passover—that it was a very special time, a time to celebrate the Jews becoming free. Never was the city more crowded or more festive! And at no other time did food taste so wonderful!

The Passover Feast, which lasted two days, was everything Jesus had hoped it would be—and much more! He met many interesting people. He discovered many new kinds of food. He wandered down many unfamiliar streets.

Finally, it was time to return to Nazareth. Joseph, Mary, and the other grown-ups packed up their

donkeys, camels, and horses and climbed into the saddles. Most of the children, still excited from all the festivities, chose to run, hop, and skip alongside the group.

Joseph and Mary figured that Jesus was running, hopping, and skipping along with the other children—but they were wrong. Jesus had stayed behind in Jerusalem!

They didn't realize this until they had stopped to rest for the night near a babbling brook.

"Have you seen Jesus?" Mary asked a neighbor. The neighbor shook her head.

"Have you seen Jesus?" Joseph asked a relative. The relative shook his head.

After getting the same response from several other people, Mary and Joseph began to feel nervous. "Maybe we should ask the children," Mary suggested. So they did.

"I haven't seen Jesus since yesterday," said a boy.

"Me neither," said the boy's sister. The other children just shook their heads sadly. No one had seen him.

"He must still be in Jerusalem," Joseph said to Mary. "Let's go back."

"But how will we ever find him in such a big city?" Mary said.

Though they were exhausted, Joseph and Mary had no choice. They climbed on their donkey and traveled back to Jerusalem. It was dark when they arrived, but that didn't stop them from searching for Jesus. They wandered up and down streets, but had no luck.

The following morning, they began to visit the homes of the people Jesus had met. Since Jesus had met hundreds of new people, this took three long days! The people were as nice as could be, offering Joseph and Mary food and places to sleep, but none of them had seen Jesus.

Suddenly, Mary noticed the temple just up ahead. "We must stop there and pray to God," she said. "We must tell him how sorry we are that we've lost his Son."

"You're right," Joseph said, sadly. They went to the temple where the

Jewish people worshiped on the Holy days, which happened to be very crowded just then.

"Excuse me," Mary said to a man with a beard. "Why are there so many people here?"

"Shhh," the man said. "We're teachers and we're here to learn." Then he turned away and stood on tiptoe to see over the heads of others. Another teacher was asking a very important question.

Someone in the center of the crowd began to answer that question in a voice Joseph and Mary recognized. It was Jesus' voice!

"How did a young boy get to be so wise?" a woman said to Mary, but Mary was too stunned to answer her.

"Excuse us," Joseph said, leading Mary through the crowd. "Excuse us, excuse us, excuse us." When they reached the center of the room, they couldn't believe their eyes. For there they saw that it was twelve-year-old Jesus who everyone had come to see!

They listened with amazement as the teachers asked Jesus complicated questions about the world. And they listened with astonishment as Jesus gave them the answers!

Finally, when she couldn't wait any longer, Mary made her way to where Jesus sat. "Mother!" he said, with a smile.

"Why have you treated us like this?" Mary cried, wondering how Jesus could be so calm. "Your father and I have been searching everywhere for you. We were so worried."

"But why?" Jesus asked innocently. "Didn't you know I would be in my father's house?"

"But my house is in Nazareth," said Joseph, who was now at Mary's side.

"Not your house," Jesus said, trying to explain. "My father's house. God's house. I'm doing God's work."

Suddenly, Joseph and Mary understood. They realized that Jesus, like God, knew more than anyone else. They had to give him the freedom to help people. They found some seats and listened proudly as Jesus continued talking to the teachers.

Finally, after Jesus had answered every single question, he returned with his parents to Nazareth. From that day on, Jesus made sure to obey his parents. And Mary and Joseph made sure to remember that they had a very special son.

If I Can Stop One Heart From Breaking

by Emily Dickinson

If I can stop one heart from breaking,
I shall not live in vain;
If I can ease one life the aching,
Or cool one pain,
Or help one fainting robin
Unto his nest again,
I shall not live in vain.

Verses on Forgiveness

If your enemy is hungry, feed him; if he is thirsty, give him something to drink. . . . Do not be overcome by evil, but overcome evil with good.

ROMANS 12:20–21

Do not gloat when your enemy falls; when he stumbles, do not let your heart rejoice.

PROVERBS 24:17

But love your enemies, do good to them, and lend to them without expecting to get anything back. Then your reward will be great. . . . Be merciful, just as your Father is merciful.

LUKE 6:35–36

Be kind and compassionate to one another, forgiving each other, just as in Christ God forgave you.

EPHESIANS 4:32

The Lord's Prayer

Our Father, who art in heaven,
hallowed be thy Name;
thy kingdom come, thy will be done,
on earth as it is in heaven.
Give us this day our daily bread.
And forgive us our trespasses,
as we forgive those who
trespass against us.
And lead us not into temptation,
but deliver us from evil.
For thine is the kingdom, and the power,
and the glory, for ever and ever.

Amen.

The Pharisee and the Publican

One day, as he did every morning, a Pharisee rose from his bed and stretched his arms and legs, looking forward to his daily routine. He walked down to the village marketplace, as he ordinarily did, his sandals flopping up and down with the same energy that you could see in the man's face.

Glancing from side to side, he strolled by the stands of various merchants and money changers, standing tall. He puffed his chest out and said aloud, "I thank God that I am righteous, not like other unjust and unfair men!" He grinned to himself. "I fast twice a week, I donate a tenth of my earnings to charity, and I never cheat men in my business dealings."

A young tax collector heard this, and without looking up at heaven, beat his chest and said, "Forgive me God, have mercy on me, a sinner." And whom do you think walked away with God's grace? It was the tax collector who had the heart to have humility before heaven—not the Pharisee who looked down upon all others.

> For everyone who exalts himself will be humbled, and he who humbles himself will be exalted.
>
> LUKE 18:14

Amazing Grace

A - maz - ing __ grace, how sweet the sound That

saved a __ wretch like __ me. _____ I

once _____ was __ lost but now am found; Was

blind but ____ now I see. _____

2. 'Twas grace that taught my heart to fear,
And grace my fears relieved;
How precious did that grace appear
The hour I first believed!

3. Through many dangers, toils, and snares,
I have already come;
'Tis grace hath brought me safe thus far,
And grace will lead me home.

4. The Lord has promised good to me,
His word my hope secures;
He will my shield and portion be
As long as life endures.

5. And when this flesh and heart shall fail,
And mortal life shall cease;
I shall possess within the veil
A life of joy and peace.

The Serenity Prayer

*God grant me the serenity to
accept the things I cannot change,
courage to change the things I can,
and wisdom to know the difference.*

Jesus' Miracles

hen Jesus was thirty years old, he traveled throughout the land to spread the word of God. During his journey, he adopted twelve very good followers (better known as his disciples) whom he could always count on for help. Jesus gave them the power to drive out evil and to heal the needy. The disciples knew Jesus was God's special Son—for they had seen him make miracles happen!

JESUS FEEDS THE FIVE THOUSAND

One day, Jesus sat in a shady meadow giving lessons to five thousand people of all ages. Everyone was so excited by what they were learning, they didn't realize that it was getting late. Finally, Jesus' friend Philip approached him.

"Jesus," Philip said, "these people must be hungry after sitting all day. Tell them to go back to their villages to get food."

"These people don't have to go anywhere, Philip," Jesus said. "Why don't you feed them?"

"Me?" Philip said, staring at Jesus as if he were crazy. "It would take me many months to earn enough money to feed all these people!"

"I have five loaves of bread and two fish," said a little boy who had overheard them talking.

"You heard the boy," Jesus said to Philip. "Bring me the bread and fish he has offered and I'll make sure no one starves."

Philip brought Jesus the five loaves of bread and two fish and watched as he closed his eyes and thanked God for being so generous. Then, in front of everyone, Jesus broke the five loaves into thousands of pieces and then divided the two fish into thousands of portions!

The people ate and ate until their stomachs were satisfied. When no one could eat another bite, Jesus asked his friends to collect the leftovers. Everyone was doubly amazed that the leftovers—from five loaves of bread and two fish—filled twelve large baskets!

JESUS WALKS ON WATER

After the five thousand people had their meal, Jesus told them all to go home. Then he turned to his disciples. "Go back to the boat without me," he said, for they had come from the opposite shore. "I'll catch up with you later."

Jesus then climbed the nearest mountain. When he reached the top, he began to pray to God. He prayed and prayed until the sky grew dark.

By then, the rowboat was already a far distance from shore. All of a sudden, the wind switched directions and beat against the small boat. Though the disciples rowed with all their might, they didn't get very far. They just bobbed up and down, up and down in the same place. Next it began to rain, and then pour. The disciples were scared!

"Help!" the disciples cried loudly. They didn't think anyone would hear them. But they were wrong. Jesus heard them! So he hurried down the mountain, raced over to the shoreline, and then he walked across the water toward the rowboat!

"I see a ghost!" cried Peter, for it was too dark and stormy for him to recognize Jesus. "It's walking on water!" He and the others shivered with fear.

"It's me, Jesus!" called Jesus. "Don't be afraid!"

The disciples recognized Jesus' voice but they were still afraid. For everyone knew it was impossible to walk on water.

"Jesus, if it's you," Peter said bravely, "then tell me to walk to you on the water."

"Okay, then," Jesus said, "walk to me on the water."

Peter climbed out of the boat and took a shaky step, and then another step. He, too, was walking on water! But when he heard the wind howl, he became afraid again. "Lord, save me!" he cried as he started to sink.

Jesus grabbed Peter's hand. "Why did you get scared?" he asked, looking into Peter's eyes. "You stopped trusting me."

Peter knew Jesus was right.

Jesus and Peter climbed into the boat. As soon as they began to row, the wind died down and the rain stopped. When they reached the opposite shore, the disciples spread word about the miracle.

JESUS HEALS A BLIND MAN

One day, Jesus was passing through the small village of Bethsaida when a group of people approached him. They had heard that Jesus of Nazareth was God's Son and that he performed miracles.

"Please, Lord!" said a woman, bringing a blind man to Jesus' side. "Can you heal our friend?"

"We heard you can heal the sick," said a man. "So we're counting on you."

The others just looked at Jesus hopefully.

Jesus took the blind man by the hand and, while the people watched, led him several feet away. Then he let go of the man's hand.

The man heard Jesus spit and rub his hands. He felt the wet warmth of Jesus' hands against his eyelids. It felt wonderfully soothing!

"Open your eyes," Jesus said kindly.

The man did as he was asked.

"Do you see anything?" said Jesus.

The man moved his head from side to side, up and down. "I see moving shapes," he finally said.

Again, Jesus placed his hands on the man's eyes.

"Now open them," Jesus said.

The man opened his eyes and shouted with excitement, "I CAN SEE!" He smiled at the rich colors around him. He was amazed by the birds in the sky, the fruit on the trees, the texture of the ground, and—most importantly—the smiling faces of his friends.

"Thank you! Thank you! Thank you!" he cried, as he threw his arms around Jesus. "You truly are the maker of miracles!"

JESUS MAKES LAZARUS RISE FROM THE DEAD

Whenever Jesus went to Jerusalem, he always stopped along the way to visit his friend Lazarus. Lazarus, also a Jew, lived in the town of Bethany with his sisters Mary and Martha.

One day, Mary and Martha sent Jesus a message. COME QUICKLY! LAZARUS, THE FRIEND YOU LOVE, IS VERY SICK. They were sure Jesus could heal their brother, and they knew he would come right away.

But Jesus didn't come right away. He knew God had made Lazarus sick for a good reason so he didn't leave till a few days later.

When Jesus didn't show up right away, Mary and Martha were terribly disappointed.

"Where in the world is Jesus?" Mary cried, bursting into tears.

"It's not like him to ignore our message," Martha sobbed.

Feeling totally helpless, they watched as their brother grew weaker and weaker.

Jesus arrived at Mary and Martha's house a few days after he got the message—but he was too late. Lazarus had already died.

"Don't worry," Jesus said to the sobbing sisters. "Lazarus will rise again."

Mary and Martha stared at him in disbelief. They didn't understand what he meant.

"He who believes in me will never die," Jesus explained calmly. "And you know your brother believed in me."

Mary and Martha continued to stare at Jesus—this time with horror. Though they didn't say this, they thought he was crazy!

"Lord!" Mary cried, throwing herself at Jesus' feet. "If you had come sooner, our brother wouldn't have died!"

She and her sister began to sob uncontrollably.

"Where have you laid your brother?" Jesus finally asked.

"Come with us," said Mary, and she and her sister led Jesus out of the house. As they walked down a stony path, they were joined by several neighbors who had also liked Lazarus. Finally they came to a cave at the edge of the woods. A large stone blocked its entrance.

"Move the stone away," Jesus said to two men with beards, and the men did. As soon as they rolled the stone away, Jesus went to the cave entrance and shouted as loudly as he could, "LAZARUS, COME OUT OF THE CAVE!"

The crowd watched in stunned silence as a strange, white figure hobbled out of the cave. It was covered in bandages from top to bottom.

"Mary, Martha," Jesus said to the two sisters, "unwrap the bandages and cloths so that Lazarus can once again be free."

With trembling hands, Mary and Martha began to unwind the bandages and cloths. First Mary recognized their brother's arm. Then Martha recognized his eye. And soon Lazarus stood right in front of their eyes as healthy and happy as ever!

"He's alive!" Mary and Martha shouted, throwing their arms around Lazarus. The crowd cheered.

"It's nice to see you again," Jesus said, putting his arm around Lazarus' shoulders.

"It's nice to see you too," Lazarus said warmly. "We have a lot of catching up to do." ✳

Story Time

The Bible contains the greatest stories ever told. Let your children create some props and costumes and gather friends for a lively story time.

Jesus' Miracle Fish
long strip of paper, scissors, markers

1. Fold paper back and forth in 1-inch segments.
2. Draw the outline of a fish on the top fold. Extend the mouth and tail to the edges so fish will remain connected when cut.
3. Cut out and unfold during story time to reveal many fishes from one.

Joseph's Coat
several different colored oblong silk scarfs

1. Tie the corners of two scarves together with a small knot.
2. Continue connecting scarves together until the colorful "coat" is wide enough to wrap around a child's shoulders and tie loosely under the neck. (Scarves should fall "vertically" from shoulders.)

King David's Crown
colored paper, scissors, aluminum foil, glue, cotton balls, stapler

1. Cut a strip of paper 6 inches wide and long enough to wrap around your child's head.
2. Paste aluminum foil on top of paper for a silver crown.
2. Make wide zigzag cuts along top edge of paper for the crown's top.
3. Glue cotton balls along the base.
4. Cut out oval and diamond "jewels" from colored paper and glue on.
5. Overlap the ends and staple together.

When much people were gathered together, and were come to him out of every city, he spake by a parable.

LUKE 8:4

Footprints

by Margaret Fishback Powers

One night I dreamed a dream.
As I was walking along the beach with my Lord.
Across the dark sky flashed scenes from my life.
For each scene, I noticed two sets of footprints in the sand,
One belonging to me and one to my Lord.

When the last scene of my life shot before me
I looked back at the footprints in the sand.
There was only one set of footprints.
I realized that this was at the lowest
And saddest times of my life.
This always bothered me
And I questioned the Lord about my dilemma.

"Lord, you told me when I decided to follow You,
But I'm aware that during the most troublesome
Times of my life there is only one set of footprints.
I just don't understand why when I needed You most, You leave me."

He whispered, "My precious child, I love you and will never leave you
Never, ever, during your trials and testings.
When you saw only one set of footprints,
It was then that I carried you."

Verses on Faith

But blessed is the man who trusts in the Lord, whose confidence is in him. He will be like a tree planted by the water that sends out its roots by the stream. It does not fear when heat comes; its leaves are always green. It has no worries in a year of drought and never fails to bear fruit.

JEREMIAH 17:7

Trust in the Lord with all your heart and lean not on your own understanding.

PROVERBS 3:5

Everything is possible for him who believes.

MARK 9:23

If you have faith as small as a mustard
seed, you can say to this mulberry tree,
Be uprooted and planted in the sea, and
it will obey you.

LUKE 17:6

317

Joyful, Joyful, We Adore Thee

Joy - ful, joy - ful, we a - dore Thee, God of glo - ry,

God of love; Hearts un - fold like flow'rs be - fore Thee,

hail Thee as the sun a - bove. Melt the clouds of

sin and __ sad - ness; drive the dark of doubt a - way; Giv -

er of im - mor - tal glad-ness, fill us with the light of day.

2. All thy works with joy surround thee, Earth and heav'n reflect thy rays,
   Stars and angels sing around thee, center of unbroken praise;
   Field and forest, vale and mountain, Flowery meadow, flashing sea,
   Chanting bird and flowing fountain, Call us to rejoice in thee.

318

The Last Supper

ne day, Jesus' disciples, John and Peter, approached him.

"As you know, Lord, tomorrow evening is Passover," said John.

"We've come to ask where you'd like to have the Passover Feast," said Peter.

"Go to the city of Jerusalem," Jesus said. "There you will meet a man carrying a jug of water. Follow him to his house, and ask the owner, 'Where may our Lord, Jesus, eat the Passover meal with his disciples?' He will then take you upstairs to a large, private guest room with a long, low table and thirteen cushions around it. That's where we shall celebrate Passover."

Peter and John went to the city of Jerusalem and did as Jesus had asked. Sure enough, they met a man who brought them to a private room as Jesus had said.

The following evening, Jesus and the other ten disciples joined them at the house in Jerusalem.

Everyone admired the serene room and the elaborately set table. As the disciples seated themselves on the comfortable cushions around the table, Jesus took a seat at one end. Just as he was about to speak, an argument broke out at the other end of the table.

"I am!"

"No I am!"

"YOU ARE NOT! I AM!"

Jesus frowned, for he knew what was going on. His disciples were fighting about which of them was the greatest and most powerful disciple. Some thought it was John; others thought it was Peter.

"Only kings and rulers fight over who has more power," Jesus said. "Don't lower yourselves. Remember, the one who serves should be your leader." Then, to everyone's surprise, Jesus began to serve the meal.

Once everyone had been served, Jesus filled a bowl with water. Then he removed his robe and tied a towel around his waist. "Slip off your sandals," he said to his disciples, "and I shall wash your feet."

Surprised by Jesus' strange request, the disciples removed their sandals. They watched as Jesus slowly made his way around the table. He knelt before each disciple, washed and dried his feet, and moved on to the next disciple.

"What are you doing, Lord?" Peter cried, just before his turn. "Washing and drying feet is a slave's job, not yours!"

"Let me wash your feet now, Peter," Jesus said calmly. "I'll explain why later."

"I'm not going to let you wash my feet," Peter said stubbornly.

"Then you'll never grow any closer to me than you already are," Jesus said.

When Peter heard this, he

321

quickly changed his mind! "Please, Lord," he begged, "wash my feet...and my hands...and my head! I may not understand why you're acting like a slave, but I do know I want to be closer to you."

After Jesus washed Peter's feet, he put on his robe, sat down at the head of the table, and looked around at his disciples. He loved each of them dearly; they were his twelve closest friends! And he knew they would carry on his work after he died.

"Now I'll tell you why I acted like a slave," Jesus finally said. "I wanted to set an example. If I, your Lord, have washed your feet, then you should do the same for each other. Remember: The servant is not better than his master. In order to be truly great, you must serve each other, not fight. I suggest you start now, for I will not always be here to remind you."

The disciples listened to Jesus with respect. They knew that as long as they obeyed him, they would be safe.

"Now I have something to tell you," Jesus said in a solemn voice. "This is going to be my last supper with you, for one of you is going to soon betray me."

The disciples gasped with disbelief! Who, they wondered, would turn their beloved Lord over to his enemies?

"Yes, it's true," Jesus said, holding up a piece of bread. "I'm going to dip this bread. Whoever dips his bread with mine is the one!"

Jesus dipped his bread in a bowl—and so did Judas Iscariot! The other eleven disciples were very surprised.

"Then go and do what you must," Jesus said to Judas Iscariot, and handed him the bread. Judas quickly left the room.

No one dared say a word, for they were horrified at what had happened. But Jesus remained calm. He picked up a loaf of bread, thanked God for it, and tore it into chunks. Then he gave a chunk to each of the remaining disciples. "Take this bread," he said, "and think of it as my body."

Next, he picked up a cup of wine, thanked God for it, and passed it around the table. "Sip this wine," he said, "and think of it as my blood."

When all eleven disciples had eaten their bread and sipped from the wine cup, Jesus continued to speak. "I will never again drink wine," he said, "until I drink it in the kingdom of God, my Father. But there's no need to be afraid. Now that you've eaten my body and drunk my blood, I will always be with you."

Angels Watching Over Me

All night, all _____ day,
When at night I go to sleep,

an - gels watch - in' o - ver me, my Lord. ____
an - gels watch - in' o - ver me my Lord. ____

All night, all _____ day,
Pray the Lord my soul to keep,

an - gels watch - in' o - ver me.
an - gels watch - in' o - ver me.

A Child's Evening Prayer

by Samuel Taylor Coleridge

Ere on my bed my limbs I lay,
God grant me grace my prayers to say:
O God! preserve my mother dear
In strength and health for many a year;
And, O! preserve my father too,
And may I pay him reverence due;
And may I my best thoughts employ

To be my parents' hope and joy;
And O! preserve my brothers both
From evil doings and from sloth,
And may we always love each other
Our friends, our father, and our mother:
And still, O Lord, to me impart
An innocent and grateful heart,
That after my great sleep I may
Awake to thy eternal day!

      Amen.

Holy Lullaby

Sleep, baby, sleep.
Thy father guards the sheep;
Thy mother shakes the dreamland tree,
Down falls a little dream for thee:
Sleep, baby, sleep.

Sleep, baby, sleep.
The large stars are the sheep;
The little stars are the lambs, I guess;
And the gentle moon is the shepherdess:
Sleep, baby, sleep.

Sleep, baby, sleep.
Our Saviour loves His sheep;
He is the Lamb of God on high,
Who for our sakes came down to die:
Sleep, baby, sleep.

For he will command his angels concerning you to guard you in all your ways.

PSALM 91:11

Verses on Angels

See, I am sending an angel ahead of you to guard you along the way and to bring you to the place I have prepared.

EXODUS 23:20

Praise the Lord, you his angels, you mighty ones who do his bidding, who obey his word.

PSALM 103:20

The angel answered, "I am Gabriel. I stand in the presence of God, and I have been sent to speak to you and to tell you this good news."

LUKE 1:19

331

Easter Peace

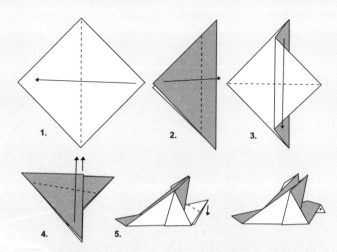

1.

2.

3.

4.

5.

Jesus came and

stood among them

and said, "Peace be

with you!"

JOHN 20:26

Celebrate the miracle of Easter by sharing the message of peace with your family and friends. With a few simple folds, your children can transform a piece of paper into a dove of peace. Make a whole flock and send them out into the world.

Dove of Peace
square sheet of paper, pen

1. Fold the square on the diagonal, matching opposite corners.
2. Fold 3/4 of the top layer back open.
3. Fold the paper in half, along the opposite diagonal. The fold from step 2 should peek out from the inside. This will become the dove's head.
4. Fold 3/4 of the top layer up at a slight angle. Repeat with the bottom layer to make wings.
5. Fold the tip of the dove's head to one side and make a crease. Open the crease, and invert the fold inward. This becomes the dove's beak.
6. Add dots for eyes and messages on the wings.

The Resurrection

fter the Last Supper, Jesus and his disciples (now only eleven of them) walked to an olive garden to rest and pray.

"What are we doing here?" John asked Jesus.

Before Jesus could answer him, the group saw lights coming toward them from the other side of the garden. Soon they could see that the light came from torches held by a group of priests and soldiers. These men, who also carried clubs and swords, were Jesus' enemies! The disciples were afraid.

"Look!" Peter whispered to John. "There's Judas!"

Sure enough, Judas Iscariot, the twelfth disciple, was coming toward them with Jesus' enemies. Only moments before, Judas had said to the priests, "Arrest the man I kiss."

When Judas saw Jesus, he walked up to him. Judas kissed Jesus, and instantly, Jesus was arrested by two soldiers.

"Leave him alone!" Peter shouted, waving his sword in the air and slicing off a soldier's ear.

"Put that sword away, Peter!" Jesus cried. "If I wanted to fight back, I would have called on God. But I know my Father wouldn't want that. He has other plans for me."

Feeling ashamed, Peter dropped the sword and returned to the other disciples. They watched helplessly as Jesus was taken away.

Jesus was pushed and shoved and dragged all the way to the high priest's palace, where the rest of his enemies were waiting.

"Tell us if you are the Christ, the Son of God," the high priest said to Jesus.

"Yes, I am," Jesus said calmly. "And one day you will all see me sitting on a throne next to God."

"He's lying!" Jesus' enemies yelled angrily. "He's not the Son of God!" But before they could have him killed, they had to bring him to the governor, Pontius Pilate.

"This man should be killed," the priests and the soldiers cried when they reached Pilate's palace.

"What has he done?" Pilate asked curiously.

"He says he's the King of the Jews," answered a chief priest.

"He makes the Jews fight against our people," said a soldier.

"Are you the King of the Jews?" Pilate asked Jesus.

"People call me that," Jesus said, "but my kingdom is not of this world. I am a King who brings truth to everyone he meets."

Pilate looked at the priests and soldiers. "I can't have this man killed," he said. "He hasn't done anything wrong."

"But all he does is cause trouble," pleaded Jesus' enemies.

"Then have King Herod make the

decision," Pilate said. So they brought Jesus to King Herod, who was in Jerusalem for the Passover Feast.

"I've heard so much about you!" King Herod said when he met Jesus. "How do you make miracles occur?" Jesus did not answer him.

"He's dangerous!" yelled a soldier.

"He should be killed!" yelled a priest.

"Send him back to Pilate," King Herod said, "I have no time for fools like him." So once again, Jesus was taken back to Pilate.

Now Pilate knew that Jesus hadn't done anything wrong. He knew that the priests and soldiers were just jealous of him. So after much thinking, he came up with an idea.

Every Passover, the people were allowed to let one prisoner go free. This year, there were only two prisoners—innocent Jesus and a murderer named Barabbas. So when the right time came, Pilate asked the crowd: "Whom would you like me to set free—Barabbas or Jesus?"

"Barabbas! Barabbas!" shouted the people. "Set Barabbas free!'

"Then what shall I do with Jesus?" Pilate asked with surprise.

"Crucify him!" the crowd yelled.

"But he hasn't done anything wrong!" Pilate shouted, hoping to change peoples' minds. But it was no use. "Crucify him! Crucify him!" the crowd yelled.

The soldiers took off Jesus' clothes and dressed him in a scarlet robe. Then they placed a crown of thorns on his head and a walking stick in his right hand. The crowd laughed and made fun of Jesus.

"Now he really looks like a king!" a soldier yelled.

The people made faces at him and spat at him. They bowed down to him—as a joke, of course.

But Jesus stayed calm. He refused to fight back.

"Jesus did nothing wrong!" Pilate cried, once again hoping to change the peoples' minds. "And I have the power to set him free!"

"No you don't," Jesus said to Pilate. "Only God has the power to set me free."

And then it was time for Jesus to be crucified.

"Carry these to the top of the hill," said a soldier, handing Jesus two large pieces of crossed wood. The wood was so heavy, Jesus collapsed underneath it! When he got up, he was weak and tired. The soldiers laughed at him and gave the cross to a man named Simon to carry uphill.

Up, up, up they went—Jesus, Pilate, the high priests, the priests, the soldiers, and the people. At the top of the hill, a priest offered Jesus some drugged wine. "It will ease the pain," he said. Jesus took one sip and refused to take another.

The soldiers began to stretch Jesus onto the cross, nailing his hands and feet to the wood. Above his head, they attached a wooden sign: THIS IS JESUS, THE KING OF THE JEWS. Then they raised the cross and buried its bottom in the dirt.

"If you are the Son of God, come down from the cross!" someone shouted.

But Jesus didn't budge. He just looked out at the crowd. He recognized a few people who were not his enemies—a woman named Mary Magdalene, his mother Mary, and his disciple John.

"Mother!" Jesus cried. When Mary looked up with tearstained eyes, Jesus said, "John is your son now."

Then he said to John, "My mother is now your mother."

After six hours, Jesus prayed to God. "Why have you done this to me?"

And for the first time in Jesus' life, his Father didn't answer. Soon Jesus began to feel pain, which became worse and worse as the minutes passed. It wasn't his pain alone. He was feeling the pain of all the sinners in the world and suffering for them.

"Father, here is my spirit!" Jesus finally cried. "It is finished!" Then he bowed his head, took his last breath, and died.

Soon after that, a rich man named Joseph took Jesus' body down from the cross and wrapped it in clean cloths. Then he laid Jesus in a tomb and sealed it tight.

Pilate sent his two strongest guards to watch over the tomb—the high priests and soldiers insisted on this. "Just in case Jesus' disciples come to steal the body," they said. "They'll want us to think that Jesus has risen from the dead!"

Three days after Jesus died, Mary Magdalene and a few other women returned to the tomb with perfumes and ointments to spread on Jesus' body.

"How will we get past the guards?" a woman asked.

"I don't know," Mary Magdalene said, "but we'll find a way."

Suddenly, the ground shook and knocked the two guards down. Then an angel appeared before the women.

"Don't be scared," the angel said. "God has sent me. I know you're here to find Jesus, but he isn't in his tomb."

The women gasped with shock. "Then where is he?" they asked.

"He has come back to life again, just as he knew he would. Come see for yourselves."

As if in a dream, the women followed the angel to Jesus' tomb and slowly entered the cave. It was empty!

"Jesus is gone!" Mary Magdalene cried. "They've taken him away!"

"No one has taken him,"

the angel said kindly. "He's risen from the dead. Tell his disciples to meet him in Galilee." Then the angel disappeared.

The women hurried away from the tomb in search of Jesus' disciples. Mary Magdalene returned to the tomb and cried. She didn't know what to believe. Had the angel been a dream? Had someone stolen Jesus' body?

Suddenly, Mary Magdalene felt someone approach. She looked up and there, before her eyes, stood Jesus!

"Oh, teacher!" Mary Magdalene cried, and knelt before Jesus.

"You can't touch me yet, Mary," Jesus said kindly, "for I still need to go to God. But please tell my disciples that I will be back." Then he disappeared.

Mary Magdalene hurried to Galilee to share the news with Jesus' disciples. Now she knew that the angel hadn't been a dream, and that Jesus' body hadn't been stolen from his tomb. Jesus had risen!

*For God so loved the world
that He gave His only Son,
that whosoever believes in
Him shall not perish but
have everlasting life.*

JOHN 3:16

Angels to Watch Over You

For he will command

his angels concerning

you to guard you in

all your ways.

PSALM 91:11

God's angels are everywhere. What do they look like? Make an angel with personal touches or create a clothespin one to clip over your bed.

Hands & Feet Angel
poster board, scissors, glue, glitter, foil, tissue paper, ribbon, child's photo

1. Have your child stand barefoot, with feet together on poster board, and trace to make the angel's robe. (The toes are the ruffled hem.)
2. Trace each hand on the poster board to make wings. (Keep fingers closer together.)
3. Cut out the patterns and glue the wings to the back of the robe.
4. Glue foil and glitter on the wings. Decorate the robe with tissue paper and ribbon.
5. Trim a picture of your child and glue it on top.

6. Make a halo out of a circle of poster board covered with foil and glue to back of head.

Guardian Clothespin Angel
colored tissue paper, glue, wooden clothespin, pipe cleaner, markers

1. Trim tissue paper into a 5 ½ x 5 ½-inch square. Fold back and forth in ½-inch segments.
2. Pinch the center of the folded wings. Glue the wings between clothespin "jaws."
3. Fold pipe cleaner in half. Twist the middle to create a loop halo on one end.
4. Bend the halo above the top end of the clothespin. Wrap the pipe cleaner ends around the angel's waist. Twist the ends together around the front to make praying hands. Decorate with markers.

Swing Low, Sweet Chariot

I looked o - ver Jor - dan and what did I see, ___

Com - in' for to car - ry me home! A

band ___ of an - gels com - in' af - ter me, ___

Com - in' for to car - ry me home!

Refrain

Swing low, sweet char - i - ot, _____

Com - in' for to car - ry me home!

Swing _____ low, sweet char - i - ot, _____

Com - in' for to car - ry me home!

2. If you get there before I do,
   Comin' for to carry me home,
   Jess tell my friends that I'm acomin' too.
   Comin' for to carry me home.

Refrain

3. I'm sometimes up and sometimes down,
   Comin' for to carry me home,
   But still my soul feels heavenly bound
   Comin' for to carry me home!

Refrain

Prayers

Now I lay me down to sleep,
I pray thee, Lord, thy child to keep:
Thy love be with me through the night
And wake me with the morning light.

       Amen.

Lord, keep us safe this night,
Secure from all our fears.
May angels guard us while we sleep,
Till morning light appears.

       Amen.

Now the Day is Over

by Sabine Baring-Gould

Now the day is over
　　Night is drawing nigh,
Shadows of the evening
　　Steal across the sky.

Now the darkness gathers,
　　Stars begin to peep,
Birds and beasts and flowers
　　Soon will be asleep.

Jesus, give the weary
　　Calm and sweet repose;
With thy tenderest blessing
　　May our eyelids close.

Grant to little children
　　Visions bright of thee;
Guard the sailors tossing
　　On the deep blue sea.

When the morning wakens,
　　Then may I arise,
Pure, and fresh, and sinless
　　In thy holy eyes.

Acknowledgments

Scripture taken from the HOLY BIBLE, NEW INTERNA-TIONAL VERSION®. Copyright © 1973, 1978, 1984 by International Bible Society. Used by permission of Zondervan Publishing House. All rights reserved.

The "NIV" and "New International Version" trademarks are registered in the United States Patent and Trademark Office by International Bible Society. Use of either trademark requires the permission of International Bible Society.

"The Sermon to The Birds" retold by James Baldwin. Reprinted with the permission of Simon & Schuster from THE CHILDREN'S BOOK OF VIRTUES by William J. Bennett. Copyright © 1995 by William J. Bennett.

"The Prayer of the Little Ducks" from PRAYERS FROM THE ARK by Carmen Bernos de Gasztold, translated by Rumer Godden, copyright © 1962, renewed 1990 by Rumer Godden. Original Copyright 1947, © 1955 by Editions du Cloitre. Used by permission of Viking Penguin, a division of Penguin Putnam Inc.

"The Prayer of the Little Ducks" English translation copyright © 1962, copyright © 1990 by Rumer Godden. First appeared in PRAYERS FROM THE ARK, published by Viking, a division of Penguin Putnam. Reprinted by permission of Curtis Brown, Ltd.

"Little Sunshine" retold by Etta Austin Blaisdell and Mary Frances Blaisdell. Reprinted with the permission of Simon & Schuster from THE CHILDREN'S BOOK OF VIRTUES by William J. Bennett. Copyright © 1995 by William J. Bennett.

"A Morning Song" by Eleanor Farjeon. Granted by permission of David Higham Associates Ltd.

"Garden Song" words and music by David Mallett. Copyright © 1975 Cherry Lane Music Publishing Company, Inc. (ASCAP) and DreamWorks Songs (ASCAP) This arrangement Copyright © 2001 Cherry Lane Music Publishing Company, Inc. (ASCAP) and DreamWorks Songs (ASCAP) Worldwide Rights for DreamWorks Songs Administered by Cherry Lane Music Publishing Company, Inc. International Copyright Secured All Rights Reserved.

"Here I Am, Lord" by Dan Schutte. © 1981, Daniel L. Schutte and New Dawn Music, 5536 NE Hassalo, Portland, OR 97213. All rights reserved. Used with permission.

"Morning Prayer" by Ogden Nash. Copyright © 1961 by Ogden Nash. Reprinted by permission of Curtis Brown, Ltd.

"No Difference" and "Ma and God" by Shel Silverstein. Copyright © 1974 by Evil Eye Music, Inc.

"Where Love Is, God Is" by Leo Tolstoy. Reprinted with the permission of Simon & Schuster from THE BOOK OF VIRTUES by William J. Bennett. Copyright © 1993 by William J. Bennett.

ILLUSTRATIONS

pg. 3 Frige Schotte; pg. 8 S. Beatrice Pearse; pg. 15 L. Perrault, pg. 18-19 Charles Robinson; pg. 29 Heilige Schauer; pg. 32, 58, 90, 120, 188, 224, 240, 252, 270, 298 H.R. McEniry; pg. 49-52, 57, 67, 77, 83, 123, 137, 173, 193, 196, 211, 214, 285 Maud and Miska Petersham; pg. 55 Peter Fraser; pg. 69, 73, 135, 139, 151-152, 181, 261, 305, 307, 309, 311 Milo Winter; pg. 95 Dovis M. Ward; pg. 99, 131 Maud Humphrey; pg. 127 H. Arnold; pg. 128-129 Clark C. Tourne; pg. 141 R. H. Porteous; pg. 148, 156 Ellen H. Clapsaddle; pg. 175 Harriet M. Bennett; pg. 228 Frances W. Danielson; pg. 237 N. Westrup; pg. 257, 329 Jessie Willcox Smith; pg. 262 Gustaf Tenggren; pg. 268 P. Ventura; pg. 277 Margaret Evans Price; pg. 289 Father Tinho; pg. 313 Gaffron; pg. 338 A.D. Blashfield; pg. 345 W. Hagelberg